A City of Han

Edited by Sollee Bae

FWS Publishing
773 Magok-dong apt#912
Gangseo-gu, Seoul, South Korea
Email: ficwriseoul@gmail.com
Twitter: @FictionSeoul

Publisher's Note: This is a work of fiction. Names, characters, places, and incidents are a product of the author's imagination. Locales and public names are sometimes used for atmospheric purposes. Any resemblance to actual people, living or dead, or to businesses, companies, events, institutions, or locales is completely coincidental.

Cover illustration © 2020 Alan Bao

ISBN 978-0-578-67829-0

Contents

Foreword 5

Umchina 8

Kyungsung Loop 22

Mosquito Hunters of Korea 36

Long Road 52

Playing the Blues in Seoul 73

Sojourn 98

Foreword

I was born in Seoul and have spent most of my adult years here, but it wasn't until recently that I became aware of its potential as a literary setting. And I say "potential", because it has not been featured in world literature nearly as much as other prominent cities of East Asia have been. Say Kyoto, and you will think of *Memoirs of a Geisha*. Say Shanghai or Beijing, and *When We Were Orphans* and *Midnight in Pecking* come to mind. But what of Seoul?

When I asked this question to others, their answers were surprisingly unanimous: that Seoul did not have a defining character. It was too bland. It was the quintessence of a modern metropolis, made up of concrete buildings and wide roads and a grey sky. If we were to compare it to a person, it would be that man or woman who worked for a marketing firm, dressed sensibly, and carried the last year's model of iPhone (but no older).

I don't expect this book to change that image of Seoul. I would like to embrace it, if anything, because I believe a lot can be said about this blandness and lack of colors. Seoul's architecture, exemplified by clusters of tall apartment buildings, is the embodiment of social hierarchy and pressure to fit in (*The Long Road, Sojourn*) which inevitably lead to fierce competition among its members (*Umchina*). It is also fast-paced, going through the cycle of tearing down old buildings and erecting new ones every five years—as depicted in *Playing the Blues in Seoul*, set in the international community where this transient nature of city life is especially pronounced. *Kyungsung Loop* and *Mosquito Hunters of Korea*, which are more historically rooted than the other stories, allow us a glimpse into the city's past traumas behind the fabulous, neon-lights façade.

Shot through these stories, and the different faces of Seoul they portray, is the keen sense of melancholy and emptiness that all characters seem to struggle with. And it was this particular brand of solitude and yearning that I looked for when selecting stories out of the initial pool of over a hundred submissions, because I believed that was what made this city so characteristically uncharacteristic: that feeling you get when gazing at the lights on the other side of the Han river, or the distant slopes of mountains between the walls of skyscrapers. If you have ever lived in Seoul, I am certain you know what I am talking about; and if you have not, you will after reading these stories.

This book would not have seen the light of day if not for the efforts of the following people: Brian, who went through each and every submission with a sharp eye and offered invaluable editorial feedback; Alan, who illustrated the cover art that is as gorgeous as it is personally meaningful; and lastly, the contributors who allowed me to publish their stories, and waited with patience during this long and difficult journey.

-Sollee Bae
Seoul, 2020

> Eliot Olesen

Umchina

"He had the diploma, but lacked the grades. He had the pedigree, but lacked the connections. Most of all, he lacked the suave nature of a Hyundai man, a Samsung man, an LG man—they were all the same, and everyone wanted to be one."

Min fell through the door at mid-afternoon, reeking of booze and cigarettes. His shirt was untucked and stained at the bottom. He held his tie wrapped and knotted around one hand. It took three, four, attempts to remove both of his shoes and kick them to the floorboard.

His mother came from around the corner, wearing soapy pink rubber gloves and a frilly apron. She opened her mouth to say something, then immediately shut it again and shuffled back into the kitchen. "Sit down," she told Min, reemerging with a bowl of hot soup. "You look like a mess."

Min didn't say anything. They ate soup in silence. He focused on keeping his feet firmly planted in an effort to stop the room from spinning.

"I talked with Su-ji today—Aunt Su-ji."

Here it goes, thought Min.

"You know her son, Jay."

Of course, the Samsung man.

"You know, the Samsung man," she added, for good measure. "He just got a promotion. He's a manager now—the youngest one on the team."

Min had never met Jay, but the specifics of his career were often discussed around this table. It seemed to be his mother's favorite subject these days.

"You two are the same age," she said. "He bought Aunt Su-ji the newest smart phone to say thank you."

Her friends often purchased items for themselves—purses, phones, even cars—and bragged that they were gifts from their sons. This was how they compared themselves to one another. There was even a word for it: *umchina*. Mother's friend's son.

"Thank you, Mother," Min said, rising from the table abruptly. He stumbled off towards his room, leaving his half-eaten soup and his mother at the table. He didn't have the patience to hear any more about Jay and his special career.

Min tried unsuccessfully to shake off his dizziness

as he turned on the television and fell backwards on his bed. He watched the ceiling spin around itself, hypnotizing him to sleep. By the time he woke, the room was dark, the apartment silent.

His mother didn't come to his room but once the next day. Min didn't bother to take off his headphones or put down the controller to his video games as she set his meal on his nightstand, but after a few awkward moments of standing there, she moved to stand directly in front of the television, causing Min to lose the round.

"What?"

She watched him piteously.

"I just wondered if you had any interviews this week. It's been months."

He rolled his eyes and put his headset back on, but there was no sound; the game had ended. She stared at him long and hard, probing for more before turning to leave the room.

"What would your father say?" she asked herself quietly; Min wondered whether he was meant to hear it.

The afternoon slipped into the evening, then into night. Min had never gotten up to turn the lights on. The blue glow of the television cast its reflection on every darkened surface of the room; and when he stepped into the bathroom, he nearly blinded himself. He cursed loudly, but he was reasonably sure that his mother wouldn't awaken. She still slept with earplugs, even though her husband's snoring died with him.

Min took a long shower and gave himself a close shave. He blow-dried his hair and worked sculpting wax through each lock with his fingertips. He applied deodorant and cologne and chose a pair of smart glasses from his collection. Tonight he went with the thick black Armani frames with the silver nosepiece—he was testing a theory about his choice of eyewear and was eager to see how the Armanis would fare. He dressed himself in his navy suit with a white shirt. He grabbed a dark red tie and held it tightly in one hand as he regarded his reflection in the mirror. He could stand to lose a few pounds, that was for sure. Ever since he'd finished his mandatory military service, his physical fitness had disintegrated until he was more curves than edges.

Min grabbed his keys and shut the front door quietly behind him. He rode the elevator down thirty floors, all the way to B3 and found his black BMW in the corner of the parking garage. He whipped up three levels and emerged on the darkened street level. Driving a car to Gangnam was ill-advised unless the car was expensive enough. Min's BMW was just passable as a high-end import. His mother had purchased it for him when he graduated from Cornell, which she regarded as just passable for an Ivy League. Jay the Samsung man had gone to Harvard. He had an MBA already. She frequently threatened to sell the car, but Min knew she never would. Doing so would reflect more poorly on her than him.

Thousands of flyers littered the ground in the club district and tiny dumpling tents piped steam into the street. Music, too loud to be anything but noise, flooded from every bar front. Neon lights jutted out from the ground, rising as monuments to karaoke, love-motels, restaurants, and women. This place had everything that Min could need. It was too loud, too bright, and too busy for him to be anything but a man in a suit, a man driving a BMW.

Min inched down the narrow side road as the crowd of people parted before him. Girls in the shortest skirts he'd ever seen leaned on one another, struggling to maintain balance on their towering heels. The men were dressed much like Min. Suits, ties, and luxury car keys that may or may not operate an actual car. They looked through his windows as he rolled past, but to them, Min was only a silhouette, insulated and apart.

He pulled into the narrow street behind a club called "Noise Basement" and parked in front of a Lamborghini. In his rear-view mirror, Min could watch the steady parade of people ambling through club row, but no one ventured down the side alley except to park.

Min reached next to his seat to pop the trunk before he stood up, leaving the keys in the ignition. He checked his reflection in his driver's side window and prayed that his hair would hold up throughout the night. He admired his Armani glasses and reminded himself that these glasses were likely to do the trick.

It baffled Min that people left such nice cars scattered around these back alleys, where there was no CCTV or regular police patrol. Then again, it was precisely these factors that drew Min to this alley in the first place. No one would disturb him.

Min loosened his shoelaces, one foot at a time perched on his back bumper. He laid a sheet of clean newspaper on the pavement before standing on it in just his socks. The subwoofers from Noise Basement sent a tickle up each of his legs as he reached into his trunk to procure a fine wooden hanger, which he held in one hand while closing the trunk with the other, just enough to click off the dome light.

He checked his surroundings on all sides, ensuring that he was alone and concealed. Satisfied, he removed his pants, folding them along the crease and hanging them carefully on the wooden hanger. His suit jacket followed, then his shirt and tie until he was standing next to the Lamborghini in just his boxers and undershirt. Leaning forward, he dug around in his trunk for a pair of gym shorts and slipped them on before shutting his trunk.

He delicately hung his suit in his passenger seat before resuming his place in his driver's seat and reclining all the way back. People frequently slept in their cars back here, too drunk to drive home. Some of the drivers didn't even have homes, only their luxury cars and a backseat filled with suits.

Min would much rather be sleeping in his bed at home, but he couldn't. If he left the house in the morning wearing a suit, his mother would get her hopes up. She'd make him eat a big breakfast and pray for him aloud. She'd press a good luck totem in his hand and wave him onto the elevator. Then, as had happened so many dozens of times before, she would struggle to keep a smile and speak reassuring words when he came back unemployed and defeated. It was better that she thinks he'd spent his night having fun.

Plenty of men in Seoul stayed out all night and all day. The clubs didn't close until well after the lunch hour in many neighborhoods, and the bars were always open. At least it wasn't hard to come up with an alibi.

A man younger, taller, and fitter than Min pulled a girl by the wrist down the alley where Min was parked and pushed her up against the brick wall of the neighboring building. He yelled and slapped her hard across the face. The girl slurred her words and held her face. The man kissed her mouth, then her cheek, and Min watched from behind his tinted window, an invisible eye to the couple's exploits.

Before long, the heavy bass from below lulled him into the twilight of almost-sleep. Motivational platitudes drifted through his mind and he tried not to think about tomorrow.

Min's phone alarm woke him. It was a foggy gray morning, gray as the pigeons that pecked at the residuals from the night before. Everything was still. Static hung in the air. An unusually quiet morning; the crowds had gone home early.

The car windows were wet with condensation. Min rocked his neck back and forth, denying the stiffness in his joints, and checked his hair in the rearview mirror—still perfectly coifed. The Lamborghini had left and a Range Rover had taken its place, its tall profile affording Min considerably more privacy. Surely an auspicious start to the day, he reasoned.

Min was careful not to drag his pant legs on the pavement or brush against the water droplets while he changed into his suit. He brushed his teeth with a water bottle and spit into the sewage grate. Checking his reflection one last time, Min felt a pang of anxiety in his gut. He sucked in his stomach, tucking it into his waistline, and lamented that he couldn't do something about his double chin.

Hyundai Logistics was a forty-minute drive over the Han River and into the old part of Seoul, near the West Gate. Min thought it fitting that Hyundai positioned its offices near the four gates, like pillars of a great city. All of the best companies in Korea did.

He parked in the lot and followed the instructions from the e-mail to the check-in counter, where he told the receptionist his name and retrieved his nametag. Everything was the same as last year except for the receptionist.

He sat in the waiting room alongside dozens of others and waited for his name to be called. He sat before the panel of wrinkled old executives and answered their questions about Cornell, about his military service, about how he thought America compared to Korea, which was just a code for him to discuss Hyundai's obvious superiority over its international counterparts. He was asked to account for his delayed entry into the workforce, even though it was apparent on his resume—six years of college plus a gap year. Two years of military service. Another two gap years.

He allowed himself to be shepherded to the corporate cafeteria, where he ate lunch silently alongside the other candidates. After lunch, he was assigned a group for the assembly interview. They were all much younger than he was, even younger than they'd looked last year. Min made himself sound confident and hurried to supply unique answers to each question, even when made to answer last.

The last step of the day was the English competency exam. As he had dozens of times before, he sat before two foreigners, on this day a white man and a possibly Hispanic woman, and answered their nonsense questions while they assessed his English. He'd practically grown up in the American school system, but he knew they'd probably ding him on accent or grammar. It didn't matter. Speaking English wasn't considered competitive anymore, especially against all these 25-year-olds.

At three o'clock, he stood at attention as the chief interviewer read the names of those who were to return the next day for a second interview. Min's name was not on that list. So much for the Armani glasses.

He kept his composure as he walked back to his car, reminding himself that he was still waiting on a call from Samsung Electronics, which wouldn't make a decision until the week's end.

He rested his head on the steering wheel and tried for deep breaths. Not even a second interview for this one. In nearly two years of interview after interview, he'd only scored a handful of callbacks, none of which materialized into an actual job. But the familiarity didn't take the sting out of the disappointment.

He had the diploma, but lacked the grades. He had the pedigree, but lacked the connections. Most of all, he lacked the suave nature of a Hyundai man, a Samsung man, an LG man—they were all the same, and everyone wanted to be one.

It was only 3:00pm. Min needed to clear his head before he went home. He drove to the cinema and got a ticket for the very next showing, a movie he'd already seen. He got a big popcorn and a box of gummy bears, even though he knew he was supposed to watch his weight. He sat in the back of the theater and wondered what made him so different from the characters on screen, or the actors who played them. He won-

dered what made him so different from the employees at the movie theater. More than once, he'd
thought about applying for a job at the cinema. He
reveled in the simplicity of sweeping up popcorn after
each showing or tearing tickets in half at the door.
Hell, he'd probably get to watch movies for free too.

But his mother would never allow it. Her only son,
a Cornell graduate working at the movie theater—it
would kill her. She would die of shame and Min
would be an orphan.

It was dusk when Min left the theater. He stopped
at the convenience store for some cups of ramen and
bottles of *soju.* He also stopped at the dry cleaner to
pick up his other suit to leave in his passenger seat for
his Hyundai-Mobis interview on Friday.

The sun had just set when he parked in the corner
of B3. You weren't supposed to smoke in the parking
garage, but everyone did. Min barely cracked the window, trying to get the smoke to absorb as deeply as
possible into the fibers of his suit. He looked at the
green *soju* bottles and shivered. He really didn't want
to drink today, but he forced down a couple sips and
spilled a bit in his lap. It wouldn't be believable if he
didn't at least smell like he'd been out all night.

It was well past dark when he stepped into the elevator, ascending to the 27th floor. Before he opened
the door, he untucked his shirt and took off his tie,
gripping it tightly around his fist. He mussed his
crunchy hair, easier said than done. He removed his

glasses and tucked them into his break pocket and took three deep breaths before letting himself through the door.

His mother came around the corner from the kitchen in her frilly apron, preceded by her voice.

"Where have you been? Have you been out all night again?"

She set two bowls of soup on the table, one for each of them. Min stirred at his soup, willing it to cool faster. She didn't say anything, making matters worse. She could have lectured him, reminded him how disappointed his father would be. She could have offered to help him get a job, or tried to hook him up with Jay, or Min-gi, or Hyun, or any one of her friends' sons, but she didn't. Min wished that she would. He wished that she would just yell at him, call him a loser, tell him he was unfit, stupid, weak.

But she didn't. She just brought him soup.

Eliot Olesen moved to Seoul in 2011 after completing her degrees in English Writing and Philosophy at the University of Colorado. Throughout her tenure in Korea, she worked for two chaebols, where she met the young Korean men who inspired *Umchina*. Although she loved Korea, especially her neighbors in Haebangchon, she repatriated to New York City in late 2019, where she writes full time. Although new to both, you can catch her on Twitter and Instagram @eliotolesen.

> Ron Bandun

Kyungsung Loop

"As a civil engineer I had worked on various projects out there in the frontiers, such as the colony's first thermal electric power plant and a transmitter site for Kyungsung Broadcasting Corporation. This enthusiastic young country man had a bright future ahead of him thanks in part to my own two hands."

E very day, he boarded the train and rode it around and around for hours. I would see him on the way to work in the morning and again in the evening on the way home.

Dark-skinned from a life outdoors, with a wispy beard, he was tall and strong like a Chosun ox; maybe he came here from the mountainous countryside up north. His clothes consisted of a loose-fitting robe, originally pure white but smudged by the soot and ash of urbanization, and a brimmed black horsehair hat, once worn only by civil servants but fair game for anyone now that the old ways were no longer observed.

He stuck out among the other passengers, who were clad in black suits and work clothes and minding their own business. My people are at our most civilized on a train, whereas most of those mountain people have never even been on a train before.

I was used to seeing poor villager-types come to gawk at our modest outpost, although most of them were young peasant women who wandered the markets of Honmachi, window-shopping at the department stores and dreaming of a life of dresses, of cars, and scents, but so rarely buying anything. This young man, in his early or mid-twenties, seemed enrapt with the sights and sounds of modernity: the electricity, the steam, all the people in a hurry to get where they were going.

It was the early 1930s, and I lived in Sansaka, just walking distance uphill from Keijo Station. The train travelled westward in a loop out into the countryside, beyond the ancient wall that had defined the traditional boundary of this backwoods mountain town where we had built our settlement.

The train, usually a single-car diesel vehicle running unidirectionally on a single track, took us out of the city at Seishomon, once the site of a great city gate. But the colonial government abolished much of the ancient wall system and tore down the gate, wishing to spread the power and wealth concentrated in the capital to the surrounding area and spur development. And we were seeing much progress.

As a civil engineer I had worked on various projects out there in the frontiers, such as the colony's first thermal electric power plant and a transmitter site for Kyungsung Broadcasting Corporation. And now that both projects were complete and running, my life was much easier, especially with the new train line connecting the region.

This enthusiastic young country man had a bright future ahead of him thanks in part to my own two hands.

One morning, when I caught an earlier train than usual, I saw that same passenger board at Akenri—the first train station outside the city. Akenri was a village of primitive hovels with mud-colored walls and clay-tile roofs. I could hardly believe anyone would board here with head held high, but here he got on every day, enjoying all the sights whizzing by out the window. In those days it seemed like every week there was something new to see along the tracks.

As he became more familiar with the sights, he channeled that energetic interest into reading, converting the train car into his own personal study room. He read books written in his own language, with Chinese characters I knew but could not decipher in the native configurations. One day I saw him holding a Christian Bible in English, but not yet ready to put his nose down in it. So I reached out in that language.

"You should learn Japanese," I told him.

He met my eyes, eager for the opportunity to converse with a fellow passenger.

"I hope to get into Tokyo Imperial University, where I can study it properly," he replied, in surprisingly precise, eloquent language.

"I see you on here every day," I told him. "Where are you going?"

"Around and around," he replied. "I can't stay at home all day and I can't afford an office. With the price of one train ticket I can sit here all day and think about the future."

He paused, distracted by the view out the window behind me, somewhere around Shinson Station.

"Have you ever seen so many buildings?" he said. "It truly is a new era for our nation."

I chuckled at his enthusiasm. "Someday I hope you visit my country," I said. "My name is Nishimura Hidemitsu."

"I'm Hwang-bo," he replied, moving closer to sit next to me. The heavy stench of garlic and brine hung from the rags he wore. But I smiled anyway.

"That's quite a difficult name to say," I told him. "You need a Japanese name."

"Do you have any suggestions?" he asked.

"I will call you Ushi-san," I said.

Others on the train, listening in on our English conversation, had been discussing us in Japanese.

"I heard Chosun people love their oxen so much, they treat them as part of the family and live in the same house together," one said.

From then on, I spoke to Ushi-san whenever I saw him on the train. In 1936 I moved to Enki, a growing community built on land annexed recently into the capital, to be closer to my work; so I didn't need the train as much anymore. It was nice, lots of new housing built not so close together, and not high up on a hillside. But I had no friends here. In my spare time, I studied Chosun art history, developing a keen interest in this new cultural frontier of our Empire.

It was a dustbowl out here, always either dry and dusty, or wet and windy. One rainy day, the gravel roads were too muddy for walking or cycling, so I caught the train. It was full, on account of the rain, and I barely managed to get a seat.

"Nishimura Hidemitsu-san!" the passenger next to me exclaimed in Japanese. "It has been a long time."

I squinted back at this fresh-faced man, who was wearing impeccably fashionable clothes that were just a little too tight for his massive frame. "Do I know you?" I asked him.

"It's me, Ushi-san!" he exclaimed.

"Oh . . . Hwang-bo," I replied in a calm tone, trying to encourage him to keep his voice down.

I studied his features. Not a trace of the brown-faced country boy remained in him. He was truly on course for assimilation.

I had no important work that day, so I invited him to join me for lunch. We jumped off the train at Seiko Station and walked to a nearby area known for its restaurants, and I treated him to a meal of *yakiniku* and *sake*.

We talked about everything: unattainable love, his independent studies, and his still-strong love of trains. He told me he wanted to be a train engineer and was looking to study in university in preparation for that. But I was worried he would soon be drafted for the war effort. Remembering his Bible, I suggested he apply at Yonhi Professional School, founded by Christian missionaries from the West.

I was in the mood for female companionship, so I requested the restaurant staff bring me a Chosun girl. Ushi-san asked for a Japanese girl. They found two female customers, bringing him a lovely girl who introduc- ed herself as Sakura, or cherry blossom, and I got a plain-faced girl I nicknamed "Butt Goat," the local vernacular for cherry blossom. Sakura sat on her knees and Butt Goat sat cross-legged at our sides and poured us drinks for a couple hours.

After lunch, I went to the nearest telephone and called up a friend at the college, an elderly professor of Japanese literature I knew to be kind and patient with hopeless causes. When he heard my friend had already mastered English and was working on Japanese, he was eager to meet the boy.

Soon after, the school admitted him to its program,

which put my mind at ease as I hated the thought of him shipping to the frontlines in Manchukuo or toiling in a mine deep beneath Hashima.

Life was looking up for me too. I was able to officially retire from engineering and fully embrace my dream job: procuring Chosun art for Japanese collectors. Apparently, a Japanese antique dealer specializing in celadon had come across some *onggi* pottery at a shop in Tomaku; and when the shopkeeper told him 100 yen, he heard 1000, which he thought was a fair price. After that, all shops started to raise their prices. And rather than discourage the customers, it had the opposite effect, making anything Chosun all the more exclusive and prestigious. This started a gold rush for Chosun cultural items, and my own personal collection of Buddhist art from across the peninsula was suddenly worth a fortune back in the Land of the Rising Sun, where the wealthy could properly appreciate it.

One day, I caught the train, only to run into Ushi-san with a pretty girl on his arm he introduced as Chieko. He talked about school, which was going well thanks to me. I told him my work would soon bring me back to Japan, which made him sad until I promised to return soon. He left alone at Kotokuri Station, and I took his empty seat next to Chieko.

"Hello, Sakura," I told her.

She blushed, clearly embarrassed that I remembered her from the restaurant. The others on the train had also taken notice.

"What are you doing with him?" one asked her. "He can provide you no future. Will you marry him, move into

his mud hut, ferment his lettuce, and pop out half-Japanese babies?"

Another butted in. "Once a woman is with a Cho-sun man, she never goes back to her own kind," he lectured her. "Know why? Because we don't want her back."

She stood to get off at Yayoicho Station, and I escorted her through the crowd and followed her off the train.

One of the passengers opened a window on the train. "I hope you like your *sake* cold!" he shouted as the train pulled away.

This was a Japanese area, although not a particularly nice one, not far from a prison brickyard. She led me to her home where we engaged in sexual congress.

I saw Ushi-san one final time before leaving for Japan. He was riding the train alone, reading a book of Japanese poetry. Of course he would be reading in Japanese, now that his own native language was being phased out. I gave him space, realizing Chieko must have broken his heart. I felt bad for him, but he would be better off with his own kind. Plus, she wasn't loyal enough for him anyway.

After I returned to my homeland, I stayed for a few years, glad to be back in civilization. I married and my wife gave me twin daughters, further complicating any return to the Land of the Morning Calm. But that didn't stop me from thinking about it.

After America declared war on us in 1941, my skills as an engineer were much in demand. American planes dropped bombs on Tokyo in April 1942, burning down our home and making me poor once again.

By 1944, we were concerned for the survival of our Empire. I set about to return once more to Chosun, which war had not reached.

I brought my family with me, fearing separation from them in time of war. But Chosun was no longer the dreamy little backwater colony with a bright future I remembered. War trains chugged through, carrying cargo to the frontlines in China and supplies back to the homeland, impoverishing Chosun for the good of the Empire; although they did affect residents from Japan as well, as food and fuel for cooking and heating became scarce. The trains took resources and left only soot and fumes, choking us slowly every day.

A friend who worked for the railroad put us up in a guesthouse at a dormitory for railroad employees near Motomachi Station. He wasn't using it anymore as his family had fled back to Japan, and it was clear he was planning to follow them back at the soonest opportunity.

As Japan faced heavy bombing, the people here feared it would hit us next. I worked once again in civil engineering to bombproof the city, while also continuing to collect local folk art for sale back in Japan. It was not as profitable as before, but there was much work to be done.

I got back into the habit of taking the train again frequently, but never saw that ever-enthusiastic young man I remembered. The trains were getting old and dirty. The bright promise of the Empire was fading into the past. In March 1944, they began dismantling the train line and reallocating resources for the floundering war effort. When I departed at Motomachi Station, I had to pass laborers digging out steel rails.

One paused to lean against his shovel for a moment's rest. We made eye contact. His tall, lanky frame looked like a sail pulled taut against a mast. He'd lost weight since last time I saw him, likely due to wartime rationing, but it was definitely Ushi-san. I wanted to talk, to find out how a promising future at a good local college had led him to hard labor, but seeing me he redoubled his efforts, hurriedly ripping the rail from the ground as if his life depended on it.

Ultimately, his efforts weren't enough. Japan finally surrendered to America the following year, ending the war. My homeland had suffered greatly; but Chosun, the land I had come to see as my second home, had been mercifully spared the ravages of war.

In the weeks that followed, we all held our breath and waited to see what would happen next. Many of my countrymen were already fleeing, with talk of Soviets coming in from north and Japanese colonial governments all across the continent becoming dysfunctional.

The first Americans arrived on September 8, 1945, to a dismayingly enthusiastic welcome from the locals. The Americans tried to maintain continuity in government, but it quickly became clear we were no longer welcome here. Even the locals who had helped with our colonization were finding their status ebbing.

One day I came home to find my wife outside with our two daughters crying. Strangers were moving our belongings out into the yard and office furniture into our house. I scrambled to pack our valuables and travel essentials into one big trunk. My wife and I each carried the trunk between us, our two daughters following behind.

We walked alongside the banks of Asahikawa, a stream entangled with kudzu vines, all the way to Ryuzan Station. There, we could catch a train for Fuzan, from where we would take a ferry back to our island nation. But when we entered the station, we found it in chaos, with all the ticket tills closed and the station crammed full of travelers both local and Japanese. I went to the entrance to the back offices, pounding my fists on it and demanding to see the station master.

The door opened and through its narrow frame squeezed a hulk of a man, blocking my entrance with his wide, sunken shoulders.

I waved a wad of money in his face. "You have to

fix this mess so we can buy train tickets and get out of here."

I waved a wad of money in his face. "You have to fix this mess so we can buy train tickets and get out of here."

"I'm doing what I can with the mess I inherited from the previous station master," he said unapologetically.

I recognized his voice immediately.

He was aged beyond his years by a hard life, but he was definitely the same man I had seen at a younger age dressed in white riding the train in circles, the same one I'd seen just last year laboring on the train tracks. Now he wore a black station master uniform.

"Ushi-san!" I exclaimed. "They put you in charge?"

It took a moment for him to recall my name. "Nishimura Hidemitsu," he said. "My name is Hwang-bo now, and this is Yongsan Station."

I nodded apologetically, forgetting for a moment the problems of my family standing right beside me, stranded and homeless in an increasingly hostile land. Seeing him now, I knew he would have gone far if he were only born Japanese. But what had we left for him, now that our Empire was shattered?

He noticed the trunk behind me. "I guess your time to leave has come, old friend."

I looked down in despair. "After everything we experienced together for the past half-century," I sighed. "We built you trains, bridges, hospitals, schools."

33

"You gave yourselves our country, and then you gave yourselves those things," Hwang-bo said.

He went to the vacant ticket till and gave me four train tickets for free, as one final parting gift.

I got to my hands and knees blabbering my gratitude in front of my wife and children.

"It's okay. This is not a sad moment," Hwang-bo said, helping me to my feet. "It is a new era for our nation."

Ron Bandun is a self-described "anarchaeologist." Originally from Canada, he has lived in Korea for over 10 years and spent most of those years documenting Korea's non-stop urban development. An interest in the neighborhood around Hongik University that is fast losing its character due to gentrification led him to the observation that all major changes in the area are directly related to infrastructure, particularly rail infrastructure. While tracing the original routes of the Danginri Line and Gyeongseong Loop Line, he had the idea to express this long-forgotten geography in a short fiction story.

› Ted Snyder

Mosquito Hunters of Korea

"In the event of war, there's no place for me here. You young folks come here for your year assignment, and after a few months, you think that you know everything about Korea. North Korea can't pull a new one on you. Let me tell you, that talk, 'in the event of war,' is just empty words for those of us who remain behind."

T he only remarkable feature of the Yongsan bus terminal was just how American it looked, painted in a beige that you only find on military installations, with peeling trim and tall weeds growing in the planters around it. If I'd fallen asleep on the bus and woken up when we arrived, I might have thought that I was stateside, not just minutes away from Seoul's raging center of drunken bar fights and come-ons from elderly *mama-sans*. Chuck Finlay wasn't what I expected, either. Waiting for me under the harsh light of a fluorescent tube in front of the building, he was stooped from sitting at a microscope for too many hours, wearing a faded blue aloha shirt that could've been from his time in the military, and had an olive drab bag slung over one shoulder. His face looked brittle, like old, tanned leather, set out in the sun for too long.

Finlay had been around long enough to know which bars preyed on soldiers stationed at Yongsan, places with their doors open into the night, the steady beat of music diffusing out with cigarette smoke and the smell of alcohol, hustlers standing out in front scouting for America-ns. Instead, he led me down some forgotten side street, where I got him to open up over a bowl of milky-white *makgeolli*.

I'd heard stories about Finlay. People considered him an icon in our field, a hunter of mosquitoes known for his indefatigable obsession with the disease-carrying insects of the Korean Peninsula. That, however, wasn't what drew me to seek him out when I was sent to South Korea. We military entomologists make up a fairly small community, and when I'd heard the stories about him, I knew there was something else hidden behind them, something that I wasn't being told. I wanted to find out what that was. And I had reasons of my own for looking him up.

"Didn't a Bill Lazaer work here back, say, ten

years ago?" I asked.

Finlay's eyes went to the door. His hand, trembling slightly, reached for his *makgeolli*.

"Lazaer. Funny you bring him up. Most everyone at Yongsan has forgotten about him."

Trying to appear casual, I ladled more alcohol into his cup. "I saw that back in the day he'd co-authored one of the identification keys for the mosquitoes of Korea, and I wondered what happened to him."

Finlay took a drink. "That was back when I was still in, I was the XO, and he was our civilian entomologist."

"You knew him, then? Did he end up marrying a Korean woman and retiring out here?"

"The last time I saw Bill Lazaer was ten years ago. Never seen him so angry in my life, it really shook me. He'd just come back from Camp Columbia, up by the DMZ."

The way Finlay told it, old Bill Lazaer had set out half a dozen mosquito traps. Not the zapper type that Americans hang on their back porches during the summer, but CDC light traps, which look like forest green plastic boater hats with wide, flat brims. Underneath the hat hangs a white plastic collection cup, illuminated by a light that draws in mosquitoes, and a small fan that sucks the insects into the cup. A battery, just smaller than a motorcycle battery, powered each trap, normally set on the ground nearby, attached by wires. Lazaer had put his traps up in several copses of trees around the perimeter of Camp Columbia, and all summer, he had been making weekly trips there to pick up the captured mosquitoes.

Mosquito-borne disease surveillance had been Lazaer's life for the past decade. Collecting mosquitoes, testing them for disease, and making recommendations to help keep the soldiers safe from disease transmission. Not glamorous work.

Things changed one August day when Chuck Finlay was the XO at Lazaer's unit. Lazaer showed up at Camp Columbia in his rusty, two-tone Ford pickup truck. His traps were gone.

Back in Yongsan, at the building that housed his unit, he threw a box of his mosquito collection equipment onto the lobby floor, then kicked it up against a wall. Late in the day, Finlay was the only person still around to hear.

Finlay's office was just off the lobby, and he stepped out to see Lazaer standing over the box, brooding. "You okay, Bill? Why don't you come into my office, sit down for a minute?" Finlay asked.

Lazaer shuffled into Finlay's office and sank down into a chair. He dropped a worn, olive drab medic bag, emblazoned with a red cross on the front, on to the floor. Glass vials for collecting insects clinked together inside of the bag.

Finlay looked across his desk at Lazaer and asked, "So, what's going on?"

Lazaer told him that the traps had been taken

down at Camp Columbia. He'd found them in the office of the Camp Columbia's preventive medicine chief. The way the chief told it, they'd been assigned a new commander, a lieutenant colonel fresh from Camp Lamonnier in Djibouti, who thought the mosquito traps looked too much like IEDs: Improvised Explosive Device, commonly used as roadside bombs. Apparently the commander had lost soldiers to a roadside bomb during his last assignment. He'd told the chief to pull the traps down, and the chief was just following orders.

"I need you guys to talk to Camp Columbia's commander," Lazaer told Finlay. "Maybe you can get through to him about the importance of mosquito surveillance."

"Did you get any mosquitoes before they pulled down the traps?"

Lazaer shook his head. "A few, but that's not the point."

"When was the last time we had someone get malaria out along the DMZ, or, heck, anywhere in Korea?"

"Why is that where you guys always go? Preventive medicine isn't the same here as it is in the US. Problems in North Korea can just come down south, through the DMZ. And in the event of war—"

"In the event of war," Finlay interrupted, "we'd have bigger medical concerns from combat loss, casualties from the minefields in the DMZ, and the potential of a North Korean nuclear attack. Really, for disease, we'd just issue a prophylactic dosage of doxy to the soldiers. Folks like you will be sent home." The words came out before he was even aware of what he'd said.

Lazaer looked down. "This is home," he said, softly.

Finlay's face flushed. "Look, this can't be the first time you've had this happen. You know that's the life we lead. No one cares about our work until someone gets sick. Is there any problem skipping Camp Columbia for a year? Wait until a new commander comes on board and then start it up again?"

Standing up, Lazaer said, "I guess that I just can't count on you guys for support." He picked up his surplus medic bag.

"Jesus, Lazaer, it's not that we don't—" Finlay said, and then stopped, grimacing. "Okay, I'll think about how we might be able to take this up with Camp Columbia's commander. I can't promise that I can convince him of anything. Meanwhile, I need you to consider an alternative course of action, someplace else you can put out traps."

"Thanks."

Lazaer walked through the building to the mosquito taxonomy lab, where he had transformed a corner of a lab bench into desk space years ago.

Interrupting Finlay's story, I asked, "Lazaer was an officer too, wasn't he? I mean, before he went to work there as a civilian."

Finlay snorted. "Yeah, I'd asked around when I got the assignment. The way I heard it, Lazaer had held the glorious rank of captain. He'd been one of the officers you just knew wouldn't make it. His hat was always crooked, his knees stained with dirt, and his reports a bit too blunt. Thing is, he was good at mosquitoes. The military just couldn't stand to lose him. Got him to exchange Army green for civilian duds. He'd been the XO about ten years before my time. Maybe more. I didn't ask him, but you know, word just traveled. Rumors."

"Did he have a family here? Anything outside of work?"

Finlay ladled more *makgeolli* into his cup. "Want more?"

"I'm good." I picked up the menu, glancing at the writing in *Hangul*, then used it to fan myself. "God, does it ever cool down here?"

"Just wait until the winter. Then it's plenty cold."

I wasn't sure if I was getting anywhere on the topic of Lazaer, so I decided to change tactics.

"So, what are your days like?" I asked. "Much different than Lazear's? You're in his job, now, after all."

Finlay put his elbows on the table and leaned towards me. "You've done mosquito surveillance, right? Or are you one of those lab rats that never gets dirty?"

I shrugged.

"The mosquito we care most about here is

Anopheles."

"Right," I said. "Malaria. We studied them in grad school. They breed in clean water, unlike other mosquitoes."

"The first thing you have to realize is that this isn't the US. When you come here, you have to look for the rice fields."

"Interesting. So you sort out the Anopheles from the other mosquitoes you collect, then test them for malaria, and send a report on the results to the commander for each camp?"

Finlay said, "Pretty much. I also consult on any cases of malaria here. Or when soldiers show symptoms after they get sent back home. Not really any different than Lazear." He took another drink of his *makgeolli*. "That day when Lazear had issues at Camp Columbia. I've tried to forget it about it. The last time I talked about it was when I filed the report with my commander. He chewed on me like a starved mosquito." Finlay chuckled, but the smile quickly went away. "I was worried about Lazear. I could tell when he left my office that he wasn't right. He was always high-strung. This seemed different."

Finlay went to the taxonomy lab, where he found Lazaer sitting at a microscope, looking at the mosquitoes he had brought back from Camp Columbia.

"Hey, Bill," Finlay said. Lazaer didn't look up. "I hope that I didn't sound harsh back there."

Lazaer turned a knob on his microcope, adjusting

the focux. "I'm not sure it really matters what I think."

"You know that's not true."

"I've been thinking about what you said. You were right. In the event of war, there's no place for me here. You young folks come here for your year assignment, and after a few months, you think that you know everything about Korea. North Korea can't pull a new one on you. Let me tell you, that talk, 'in the event of war,' is just empty words for those of us who remain behind." Without looking up from his microscope, his left hand picked up a second set of forceps that lay nearby. "You military, you're the ones that don't have a place here, not really. Your kind just come in, stay for a year, then move on out. Hopefully there's not too much of a mess left behind."

"When was the last time you had a vacation? I've heard that Thailand is nice. One of the guys got a place down south, on the beach, for cheap. Or then there's Bangkok, if you're into that."

"27 Anopheles from this one trap. And they don't want to continue trapping. The commander knows better than us." Lazaer leaned back in his chair, away from the microscope and rubbed his eyes. "It was last year, before you arrived. Three guard, from Missouri, went back home after their tour. Went to their family practitioner a few weeks later, complaining of flu-like symptoms. They ended up having malaria. Just because we don't have people falling out of formation doesn't mean there's not a problem here that needs monitoring."

"Right. Like I said, I'll talk to the commander in the morning. You get anything to eat on your way back this afternoon? Want to go grab a bite?"

Lazaer shook his head. "I need to get through some more mosquitoes."

Finlay looked around the lab. "Ok, well, don't stay too late, you hear?"

Wanting to say something more, he watched as Lazaer took a vial out of a box on the lab bench and wrote a small number on its side. He picked back up his forceps and took a mosquito by the leg, transferring it into the vial. Finlay watched him move several more mosquitoes, then finally left.

As for the rest of the story, Finlay deduced it from the time he had spent with Lazaer.

Lazaer knew that he could find better collection sites. He'd studied the maps for years, looking for the best places to trap. Camp Columbia was good because of its proximity to soldiers. What it lacked, however, was proximity to breeding sites. He pulled out his map of the area, picturing the terrain from his scouting expeditions for placed to collect mosquitoes. This was back before Google Earth and GPS, but he didn't need that.

Spreading out his map, he leaned over it, pencil in hand. He marked a small village within the South Korean side of the DMZ, Daeseong-dong, not far from Camp Columbia. When he had driven through the DMZ, he had seen it from the road: a small collection of buildings with bright blue roofs.

Many people think of the DMZ as a desolate wasteland, filled with minefields and tank traps. In fact, looking out over it, even from a slight elevation, visitors see that it is dense with dark green expanses of maples, poplars, fir, rolling hills that open up to lowlands with rice fields, flooded and worked by farmers in the area. In the distance, partially obscured by haze, is a chain of mountains that mark North Korea.

He knew that some of the people who lived in Daeseong-dong worked as rice farmers. He knew there must be rice fields nearby. Likely the water in the patties teemed with mosquitoes. He had often thought this was the source for the mosquitoes he caught at Camp Columbia.

The next day, Lazaer checked out the old Ford pickup while it was still dark, before anyone came in to the unit. He had a long day ahead of him. He drove from Seoul to the DMZ. The guard at the security checkpoint looked at his military ID and waved him through. On his left side as he drove, the forest seemed like a dense wall of darkness, unfazed by the weak light of dawn. He knew that somewhere, out through the undergrowth, he could find the rice fields.

After thirty minutes or more of driving, he found a spot where the morning light illuminated an opening in the forest. He looked at his map, laid out in the passenger seat. This was it. Just like he had hoped, the trees were sparse and he could get through, close to Daeseong-dong. There was even less undergrowth than he had expected. Lazaer pulled over. He turned off the headlights and killed the engine, got out, his surplus medic bag slung over his shoulder.

Early that afternoon, Finlay arrived at the same spot. The military police had cordoned off one lane. An officer stood in the road, controlling traffic in both directions. Another stood next to the old Ford pickup, waiting for Finlay.

The air had a metallic tang that Finlay didn't recognize. It seemed more like a taste in the air rather than a smell. Looking around as he walked up to the military police at the site, he could see dirt scattered over the hood and windshield of the pickup.

The military police told him that they weren't sure how Lazaer had missed it.

Looking through the viewfinder on his Polaroid, Finlay agreed. Metal stakes had been planted in a row alongside the road, knee high on an adult. Halfway down was a row of barbed wire. A coarse fiber rope was strung along the top, creating a crude fence. Lazaer would have had to step over it to get into the woods.

Northward through an opening in the trees, he could see a lowland with several rice fields.

He took several photos of the fence, including one that showed how, at intervals, maybe every ten feet or so, hung a red sign, an inverted triangle, the size of your hand. These signs, these fences were common-place in the DMZ. The red had faded from years of exposure to the sun. The black writing, however, had not. Bilingual, in Hangul and English. Each one bore a single word, in both languages: "MINE."

Finlay leaned back in his seat across from me, said, "Bottom's up," and drained his cup of *makgeolli*. "Unit had a job opening. I was rusty at mosquito ID, but that's just like riding a bike." He looked at his wristwatch. "We still have time. You like Korean girls? I have a *mama-san* not far from here that can hook us up, and no problems, if you know what I mean."

My mind was still on Bill Lazaer and I didn't re-spond right away.

Standing up, Finlay said, "Come on, captain. I've got an early day tomorrow." He slung a surplus medic bag over his shoulder. The bag's flap was pocked with small burn marks.

I finished my drink. "What's up tomorrow?"

"Setting up some new trap sites." He shrugged. "Let's go. I won't take too long, I just don't have the stamina you younger guys have."

"Where are you trapping tomorrow?"

We walked out of the bar, into the dark side street.

"You know your way back to Yongsan? I'll pay up so you can take as long as you want. I think the last bus back to Humphries is at 2 AM."

"Finlay, what are you doing?"

He stopped and looked at me, his head tilted

slightly to the left. "I'm just looking for a good time. Aren't we all?"

I didn't follow him.

My flight out of South Korea was the next afternoon. I couldn't sleep on the flight. Back in my office, I knew that I had orders for my next assignment. I was being sent to Korea, to serve as the XO for Finlay's unit.

When **Ted Snyder** arrived in Incheon, military orders in hand directing him to Yongsan Garrison in Seoul, he only knew Korea from the stories his fellow soldiers told him.

Everything changed for Ted during a trip through the DMZ. A convoy of self-propelled artillery forced him off the road, just before a bridge. The artillery were too heavy for the bridge and had to cross slowly, one vehicle at a time. Others had to pull aside, too. Most were civilians, the people who stayed behind at the military bases in Korea. Ex-soldiers who had married Korean women. Lost people who had found something in Korea that they couldn't find anywhere else in the world. And Ted heard their stories: tales about the minefields of the DMZ and of defectors risking the trip south. There, sitting alongside the road watching artillery pass by for what seemed like hours, the seed of this story was planted.

Military orders returned Ted to the United States, where he currently resides, having gone back to civilian life. While dreaming, however, he finds himself still in Asia. You can read Ted's stories in *Leaping Clear* and *Strange Stories*, and his poetry can be found in *Inverted Syntax*, *The Mythic Circle*, *Split Rock Review*, and *Mosaic*. Find out more on his website at tedsnyderonline.com.

> David Smith

Long Road

"The river glows in violent embers as the flames conduct the subtle motions of the night. The smoke continues to fill his lungs. He coughs as he stretches his hand out to the fire, imagining greater warmth. Grey flakes of ash flutter on his raised arm."

B y the time Ju-ho exits the apartment building and returns to his motorbike, the fallen snow has thinly covered the black asphalt of the street. Pale exhaust wafts around the bike and hovers in the winter air. His footprints through the snow are fresh, and his worn sneakers shift precariously on the sleet-slick ground. He reaches through the opening of his helmet and pulls his scarf up thicker around his mouth and cheeks. His breath is hot and moist against

it, and he smells cigarette smoke in its wool. He undoes the latch of
the cargo hold and fixes his case into it after the door falls open. In the faint streetlights he can see the smears of black *jajangmyeon* sauce and scattered crumbs. A car pulls along the street behind him and in the snow and exhaust he looks ethereal, a figment of the winter night's imagination; half-memory, unseen as he weaves through the arterial streets of central Seoul. He climbs onto his bike and lowers his face-mask, kicking the engine back to life. He looks up briefly before riding down the street and watches the snow fall through streetlights. His footprints behind him fill steadily, the world returning to constant white, the promise of deep black beneath.

Exiting the side alley, he pulls out onto the empty street. A taxi speeds by, the red "vacant" light shining behind the windshield. Two parallel lines carve through the snow behind it. Dead of night, mid-week, winter storms pending; the city sleeps through it. The bike idles between his legs and when he accelerates the worn tires struggle to find action through the snow. He meanders, curving and weaving through the lanes. The snow falls heavier and he feels it against his skin in the gap between his gloves and jacket, his wrist growing wet. The entrance to the highway cuts to his right and he drives on into a valley of high rises, flanked by skincare clinics and empty bus stops.

He slows to a stop at a red light and the phone

tucked into a plastic sleeve on the handlebars blinks to life.

Pick-up Apgujeong. Drop off Sinsa. He taps to accept it as a neon sign for a *noraebang* flashes from blue to orange. A familiar pit begins opening in Ju-ho's chest.

● ● ●

In the final week of military conscription training, Ju-ho and his training unit were led to a trailer at the far side of the camp. They marched through bramble and dead leaves, and the blue sky stretching over the weary men looked to be on the verge of shattering. Their training commander stood with arms crossed by the trailer's only door, a wooden crate beside him. In concise sentences he explained what the trainees would do as they each collected a mask from the box. Ju-ho felt the rubber edges of the mask and flicked the thick plastic of the goggles with his middle finger. The drill, the commander repeated, was simple: enter the room with your mask on, sit down, and take it off. Then simply wait for further instruction. For once he didn't shout but spoke calmly, almost reassuringly. The soldiers stood in a line and fidgeted. A cold wind swept through them and Ju-ho tried to trap it in his lungs.

The commander stepped in front of Ju-ho and stared at him.

"Nothing to grin about today, Private?" he asked in a whisper only Ju-ho could hear. Then the commander turned away and called out for Jin-yeop, a tall young man who had excelled throughout the training.

"I'll remain outside. Inside, Jin-yeop will be in charge," The commander said, and nodded at the young man standing at attention before stepping aside and opening the door behind him. Jin-yeop stepped through the doorway first, and the rest of the trainees followed.

The room was empty except for a square podium in the center. The goggles gave the room a sickly yellow tint, and Ju-ho's heart began to beat faster. They gathered around the podium and sat down. The commander stood in the doorway and instructed them to remove their masks and place them behind their backs. Ju-ho slipped his off and sniffed at the air, flinching away from its lingering chemical scent. The commander shut the door, and the trainees were left silent and anxious. Ju-ho looked down the line at Jin-yeop, who was kneeling with his eyes closed and hands resting calmly on his thighs. Ju-ho was about to crack a joke to ease the tension when a hollow click reverberated through the empty room. White froth began pouring from the podium's grated sides.

Ju-ho's first breath was a warning, and in another half a breath the gas stuck in his throat and choked him. From there the pain spread. Countless needles assaulted his skin, and his eyes were washed in salt.

The others collapsed in the same reaction as they began retching and crying out. The white froth covered the ground and reached up at Ju-ho's face, where tears streamed down his cheeks in torrents. Through the panic he heard someone screaming about masks as another body fell against him. Pushing the man off, Ju-ho reached behind his back for his mask but felt nothing but the cool touch of the concrete floor. He stumbled down into the gas and gagged on the poison. A clear vomit rose from deep in his chest before erupting from his mouth.

Ju-ho struggled to stand and his brain screamed for escape. Survival instinct lurched him toward the door. He turned the handle but it held tight. He coughed and sputtered and crashed against the door, budging it open as the commander pushed it back against from the other side. Ju-ho could barely make out the commander outside, yelling and swearing at him. Then Ju-ho collapsed, suffocating, lacking the air to cry out.

A hand grabbed Ju-ho's shoulder and propped him against the wall. A mask was tugged down over his head and he felt it tighten against his face. Soon the needles began to reside, and jagged breaths brought air to his lungs. The commotion around him settled to a few hacking coughs and sobs. Opening his burning eyes, he found Jin-yeop holding him up. "Slowly, breathe," Jin-yeop instructed.

Five minutes later the door opened. The last wisps of gas drifted out around the men as they crawled out into the open air.

• • •

Ju-ho smokes a cigarette outside of the restaurant where he waits to pick up the order. A few blocks away he can see the apartment complex where Jin-yeop had lived. Its cascading towers are bright and opulent against the still sky. Decorative lighting along the rooftops cast a halo against the dark. Ju-ho wonders which building it was. Could he see it from here, from this low street? The door rings open behind him and an *ajumma* hands him a bag full of *tteokbokki* and fried seafood. Steam puffs out from the black bag. Ju-ho flicks his cigarette into the snow, and its ember sputters out in the damp. He exhales smoke and packs the food onto his bike. He looks up at the apartment once more before driving away. The complex's glow shifts from yellow to pale green, then a crisp beacon of blue against the dull skyline.

He revs the throttle and speeds off toward Sinsa Station. The snowfall parts for his passing, a vessel through a sea of distant and indifferent stars.

• • •

Ju-ho spent the two years of his military conscription stationed outside of Sokcho on the northeastern coast, and Jin-yeop received the same post. Their main duty was to watch the waters for any signs of North Korean activity, and they often joked that they would be the first line of defense if an invasion ever did come. Off-duty, Ju-ho would exaggerate his vigilance and stand on the beach with his chest puffed out, skinny arms flexed, a cigarette dangling from his lips, shouting out threats to whatever maritime challenger might be out beyond the waves. Sitting on the beach, Jin-yeop would laugh at his friends and dig his feet into the sand.

At night they played rock-scissors-paper to draw first watch in the tower. As one sat at the perch, the other would slump on the floor and nap. Together they started the habit of building towers out of cigarettes, which rose in the corner of the tower's observation deck until the two picked away at them, floor by floor. The searchlight in the tower stayed unlit. Aside from the blinking lights of the consoles in the watchtower the dark was total. Ju-ho could barely make out the line of pines along the beach, and the nightly ambiance of the wilderness was buried under the soft rhythms of the waves.

But each morning the sun would crest over the distant sea, and Ju-ho and Jin-yeop would descend from the tower and smoke the last of their cigarettes watching the sunrise. Exhausted of conversation from the night of small talk and jokes they stood silently, sleep hanging heavily in their eyes, their minds puffy and imprecise from their nocturnal, quiet lives.

Ju-ho counted the ships every morning. They were only pins of light in the dark, but they gained form and purpose in the orange dawn: the fishing boats, shipping freighters, military crafts. He thought of the men on those boats, isolated in their cabins, or standing on deck underneath the radio antennae that crowned each ship, looking back toward the shore.

● ● ●

The PC room is on the fourth floor and the worker at the front desk points Ju-ho toward the section where the order was made. Looking over the cubicles Ju-ho scans the room for the recipient. A scraggly young man with wisps of a thin moustache stands up in the smoking section and waves him over.

The customer doesn't notice Ju-ho when he arrives at his station. He budges the keyboard over to make room for the food on the desk. Ju-ho drops the carrier to the floor and kneels down to empty it. As he places the order on the tabletop, he notices the man's fingers clacking away, the long uncut nails with layers of dirt beneath them. Ju-ho waits patiently as the man finishes his game. Dark circles line the man's eyes and his hair hangs over his forehead in greasy swathes. An explosion goes off over the speakers and the man swears, slamming the mouse down on the desk. He digs a ten-thousand-won note out of his pocket and places it by the food before stabbing the keyboard to start again. "Thanks," Ju-ho says. He counts out the change, picks up his carrier and leaves.

Outside he loads his bike again and sits on it. A drunken university student stumbles away from him through the neon-painted alley. The snow falls heavier as Ju-ho turns toward the river and the bridge, not checking his phone.

● ● ●

After military service, Ju-ho went back to his hometown north of Seoul while Jin-Yeop started his life in the city. Ju-ho got a job with a moving company, and his days were spent hauling refrigerators up flights of stairs and handling the countless possessions of the customers. Each night as he tried to fall asleep in his childhood bed, listening to his father shuffle around the apartment aimlessly, Ju-ho would recall the soft murmur of the waves.

It was three months later when Ju-ho received a text message from Jin-yeop, inviting him into Seoul that weekend. He read it without responding but thought about it through the rest of his workday. He had never expected to hear from Jin-yeop again, even if they had grown close during their time in the military. Though Jin-yeop never talked about himself much, Ju-ho had pieced together enough from his friend's brief comments, or the few times Jin-yeop shared a childhood story that was vastly different from what Ju-ho had experienced. There was his education around Gangnam, his family trips in America, and on top of everything, his graduation from Yonsei University. When they parted ways after the military, Jin-yeop was already set up with his career at a major company, and Ju-ho slumped back to Seoul to scrounge together whatever life he could. Reading the message again he looked up at the old men he worked with shambling around him.

This is my life now, he thought bitterly. Outside of the military, whatever link had existed between his and Jin-yeop's lives was gone. He put his phone back into his pocket without responding.

But the next week he received the same text from Jin-yeop. It said nothing of the previous message and simply invited him into the city again. *Let's meet up.*

He didn't respond until the third week after receiving another text. He had a moving job in Gangnam that Saturday. He told Jin-yeop where he would be, and that he could meet after his work was finished.

Ju-ho found Jin-yeop sitting alone at a modest barbecue restaurant in a back alley away from the subway station. Jin-yeop rose to greet him, smiling and shaking his hand as he gripped his other arm. Ju-ho ran over his prepared response once again in his head: I'm helping my father; just odd jobs for now. But Jin-yeop skipped over the catch-up chatter as they sat down.

"I was thinking the other day," Jin-Yeop said as he

started pouring shots of *soju*, "of the time the foreigners camped on our beach."

Ju-ho smiled and nodded, remembering the night, how they scattered across the sand like startled crabs when Jin-yeop lit them up with the spotlight.

"Remember the one that began dancing though? He spilt the bottle of beer in the sand?" Ju-ho asked. He stood and re-enacted the scene, grasping a bottle and slurring together a few English words, pantomiming tears as he tipped the bottle on the table. Jin-yeop laughed. The patrons at the next table glared at Ju-ho's act. By the end of the night, empty green bottles ringed their table; and they finally paid after being asked the third time by the owner to quiet down. Stumbling toward the taxi stand, Jin-yeop asked if his work would bring him back into Seoul next week.

Ju-ho shrugged. "Doesn't matter," he said. "I'll see you next weekend." A taxi pulled up and Jin-yeop opened the door for him.

"Next week then," he said. Ju-ho nodded drunkenly and climbed into the backseat, where he drifted to sleep as the taxi crossed the Han, the rising sun outlining half of the city in golden trim.

• • •

Ju-ho cuts across the intersection and winds along the road that takes him underneath the bridge. A clear line blocks the snowfall where the bridge coverage begins. His bike huffs in the quiet as he lowers the kick-stand. Hopping the small barrier, he makes his way to the water's edge. The bridge looms over him, the skeleton of its underbelly creaking in the cold air. He stands along the water as the chill creeps through his boots and into his toes. The homeless who have caught Ju-ho here over the past week are gone tonight. For a moment, no cars pass overhead and the city is quiet—except for the whisper of the passing river.

Would the water appear darker from atop the bridge, Ju-ho wonders, or was this the blackest it became, right in front of him? He smokes, staring down at the water, no trace of his reflection in the murk.

Back on his bike, he coaxes the engine up the hill toward the main road. He courses through the falling snow and reaches the entrance ramp for the highway.

• • •

After a year of heading into Seoul every weekend, Ju-ho found a small basement apartment closer to the center of the city. He would often just sleep at Jin-yeop's after a night of drinking, crashing on his couch with a bottle of *soju* tucked in his arm.

One morning, Jin-yeop woke him as he got ready for work. He smacked Ju-ho's foot and teased a half-empty bottle of beer underneath his nose. Ju-ho woke with a start and looked at his friend in amazement as a hangover erupted in his skull. "How do you do it?"

has asked through a groan.

Jin-yeop just laughed. He left first, fixing his tie at the front door as he said goodbye. A few hours later, on Ju-ho's way out, the security guard in the lobby handed him a hangover elixir that never worked.

Ju-ho got to know his friend's apartment well. The designer furniture; the spotless walls that wouldn't allow the faintest hint of black mold in the humid days of summer; the antiseptic glare of the pristine bathroom. During their nights together, they never spoke about the gap between them. Ju-ho wouldn't talk about his day of strenuous labor, and Jin-yeop said nothing of his own career. It was all old jokes, kept on a constant cycle. A story and a shot; another one-liner, another beer. But when Ju-ho returned to his own apartment, and when he explained a broken mug to another irate customer, he could think of little else than Jin-yeop in his beautiful apartment, his friend in his downtown office.

Once, over barbecue, Ju-ho got too drunk and asked about Jin-yeop's job and all the grandness of his life. He listed all the things in Jin-yeop's apartment he would never have, the opportunities he would never know, the women he could never meet. In Ju-ho's drunk memory he thought he had said it all teasingly, but he knew he was just confessing his own shame. When Ju-ho asked about his salary, Jin-yeop didn't respond.

Ju-ho poured more *soju*. "You have it all," he

mumbled into his glass.

Jin-yeop looked at him, lifted his shot in silent acknowledgement, and drank it. He filled their glasses back up and they drank until morning.

● ● ●

Taxis race by him on the highway and his bike shakes violently with their passing, but Ju-ho keeps the accelerator tight. His RPMs waver at the max and he watches the needle bounce spastically on the speed-ometer. The snow continues to fall, and the flakes melt as they hit his visor, further obscuring the already dark road. The river to his side creeps along like oil drudged up from the depths of the earth, coursing its way thickly to some ancient engine.

The bike accelerates to its absolute limit, quivering with the stress. Ju-ho plummets through the circles of streetlight at tempo, quick successive waves of pale light and shadow. He hits a slick of ice. The bike urg-es for freedom from his grasp, but his grip holds and he straightens his ride. Other cars move into further lanes, honking their warnings, but he doesn't hear them.

Ju-ho looks up and the rushing air blasts through the bottom of his helmet. A blade-like sliver of moon hangs above the buildings that line the highway. He lowers his sight back to the road where a tunnel en-trance leaks orange, hazy light into the night. He closes his eyes and disappears into the mouth of the tunnel.

• • •

At first, Ju-ho came up with excuses for not meeting Jin-yeop. In his short responses he explained how the day at work had been too demanding on him, or he was still recovering from a stomach bug. Sometimes he told him that he had left Seoul for the weekend on some imagined trip to the countryside. He agonized over his stories, typing out and deleting entire scenarios until, after months of doing so, he simply quit responding.

Jin-yeop continued to send a simple text every Friday, never more than one. *Let's meet up.* The number in Ju-ho's message notification continued to grow as the weeks went by.

Sometimes, after a few drinks in his apartment, Ju-ho would stare at his phone and will himself to text Jin-yeop back. But he'd look around his room, his drink-heavy eyelids blinking slowly as they scanned the surroundings: the dirty sheets over a stained mattress, the mold-speckled corners behind his cheap bedframe, the streaks of grease around the stovetop. He'd hear more acutely the constant, slow drip of rusty water coming from the bathroom. Then he'd think of Jin-yeop, looking out over the city from his apartment, high above Ju-ho's basement hole. The light on his phone's screen would go out, leaving him in the dark again.

Restless and unable to sleep, Ju-ho took on a night job as a delivery driver. Eventually, the weekly messages from Jin-yeop stopped.

● ● ●

He hears the sirens behind him before he opens his eyes, and loosens his grip on the accelerator. The needle on the speedometer sighs as it drops away from the extreme edge. Ju-ho squints and lets himself feel the cold air that has pierced through him. With a soaked glove he tries to wipe the moisture from his visor. He finds himself shaking from the cold and from something else. His bike quakes between his legs. He doesn't know what kept it upright.

Emergency lights flash behind him. The tunnel ends ahead of him and the night beyond the exit appears as a wall of solid black, but he breaks through it and the city envelops him again. He pulls the bike onto the shoulder and stops by the guardrail. He opens his visor and tugs the scarf away from his mouth and nose. He coughs on the smoke that has filled the air as a fire truck speeds by him, its sirens blaring.

● ● ●

When the order came up over his phone during his second week as a delivery driver, Ju-ho hesitated. It was the same apartment building as Jin-yeop's. When it came through again a few minutes later, he accepted it.

The security guard in Jin-yeop's building was the same, and Ju-ho greeted him when he entered. The guard stared at him for a second before nodding back, his mouth slightly agape.

As Ju-ho finished his delivery, his curiosity grew. He entered the elevator again and, instead of going to the lobby, he tapped the button for the 24th floor. In the hallway, everything was as he remembered: the fragrant air, the soft modern lighting, the carpet cushioning his steps. He carried his case carefully, not wanting to knock it against the wall and disrupt the quiet. He turned the corner toward Jin-yeop's apartment.

When he reached Jin-yeop's apartment, the door was wide open. Ju-ho stepped through the doorway and looked around the empty apartment. He lay his case in the foyer and walked around, finding no trace of his friend. The apartment was barren. Left in its naked state it revealed flaws Ju-ho had never noticed before. Red crayon ran along one wall, and torn wallpaper half-coated a corner of the living room. The marble in the bathroom made it feel cavernous and damp, and a thin crack began to creep across the window that looked down over the Han River.

Back in the lobby, Ju-ho asked the security guard where Jin-yeop had moved. The guard looked at Ju-ho, confused. "Do you remember me, *ajusshi*?" Ju-ho asked, thinking the guard didn't recognize him as a delivery driver.

"Of course," the old man responded. "But don't you know?"

"I haven't spoken to Jin-yeop recently."

The guard sat down and quietly told Ju-ho that Jin-yeop had thrown himself from a bridge the month before. There was no note, the old man added as an afterthought.

Ju-ho loaded the carrier back onto his bike and drove off. When his shift ended, he rode home in the twilight— back through the scratched neighborhoods of Seoul, through the back alleys that peeked in at the guts of kimbap shops and dry cleaners. A three-legged cat darted in front of him as he pulled in in front of his apartment. He sat on his bike and waited for it to hit him, but nothing did. Sunlight crept over the rooftops and flares stabbed at his tired eyes. He swung his leg over his bike and got off, and walked down the steps to his apartment. Fumbling with his keys he opened his door and slid into the dark, closing the door firmly behind him.

$\bullet \ \bullet \ \bullet$

Ju-ho walks toward the guardrail and looks down at the apartment development built up along the river. In its ordered rows of identical high-rises, one building roars, engulfed in a brilliant fire. Flames whip up its sides and immense flumes of smoke and ash spew into the winter night. The air thickens with smoke, and Ju-ho feels the burning weight of it when he inhales.

Fire trucks surround the burning building, their emergency lights dull and scant in the vibrant aura of the conflagration. The snow and ash mingle in the crackling air; and underneath everything, there's a faint hissing. The river glows in violent embers as the flames conduct the subtle motions of the night. The smoke continues to fill his lungs. He coughs as he stretches his hand out to the fire, imagining greater warmth. Grey flakes of ash flutter on his raised arm.

His phone brightens with a new order at his bike. Ju-ho looks once more over his shoulder at the burning building before saddling his bike again. He taps to accept the delivery request.

Pick up Apgujeong. Drop off Sinsa.

David Smith grew up in southeastern Ohio and graduated from Ohio University with a degree in English Literature. He came to South Korea in late 2011 and taught in a small town on Geoje-do before moving to Seoul the following year. Inspired by the scope, urgency, and potential of the city, he co-founded the writing group Frozen Garbage with a few like-minded friends. Meeting monthly, the group members shared and workshopped their short stories and helped each other develop from terrible writers to, well, slightly less terrible writers. Frozen Garbage published two short zines—From Here Moving Forward and Thrown Together—that received glowing reviews from the members' mothers. David currently works in publishing and lives in Seoul with his wife and dog. He hopes to find the time to continue writing soon. Maybe tomorrow. Or next week.

> Matthew Grolemund

Playing the Blues in Seoul

> "*My father used to say that every twelve bars of the blues is like being born, dying, and being born again. Birth, death, and rebirth, over and over again. And if you do it enough times, you learn how to make it your own. That's the blues.*"

I t happens from time to time.

On the subway, when a group of giggling university students in matching jackets push their friend, the one they must cheat off of in English class, into the empty seat beside me.

At a crosswalk, when I get stopped beside a businessman who's had just enough shots of *soju* at his company's hweshik to put the English lessons they force on him to the test.

In a coffee shop, when the barista responds to my carefully-pronounced Korean with a blank stare because she wasn't expecting to hear her own language.

At a bar, after I play a gig. Every time, without fail.

And in cabs back home, those nights when the last and first trains are both out of the question, when I learn the *ajusshi* behind the wheel also spent a small chunk of his life an ocean away from home.

It doesn't happen often, but it does happen. Koreans, who would never strike up a conversation with a stranger in their own language, want to chat with me in English. And it always starts the same way.

"Where are you from?" they ask.

"Nowhere," I answer, even though they never laugh, and I never know if they're trying to find "nowhere" on a map in their head or if I'm just not funny.

But not Ho-joon. Ho-joon gets it.

● ● ●

I'm talking to Eun-seong, my girlfriend, while on my way home from band practice with Seong-eun, my friend who is also a girl. Well, calling it band practice isn't quite fair, since the band is just me on guitar and Seong-eun on violin, but Eun-seong, my girlfriend, doesn't like it when I call us, by which I mean me and Seong-eun, a duo, or a two-piece, or any other term in

English or Korean showing a partnership between two people. What she really doesn't like is picturing me alone with another girl. It doesn't matter that Seong-eun's been practically engaged since college and they're just waiting until he finishes school and gets one of those sweet chaebol programming jobs to make it official. Eun-seong's never going to like it, kinda like I might never want to meet her parents, knowing what that often means in Korean culture. Hell – I've only been seeing her for three months. But she assures me this would be a casual meeting, not a sign that marriage is right around the corner.

"They're just—" And here my nearly-fluent girl-friend has to search for the right word— "curious."

Eun-seong is so excited about the meeting that she doesn't seem to hear when I tell her this Sunday is terrible for me. Today's already Friday and I have a gig with Seong-eun tomorrow night. That alone I could manage, but tomorrow night is also Jimmy's last night in Seoul before he moves back to England. Jimmy's the first friend I made when I moved here and he's been my closest ever since. I promised weeks ago that I'd go drink-for-drink with him until the morning trains started, just like we used to back when we met, when this whole living abroad thing was still a puzzle and I was just glad I didn't have to solve it alone. Eun-seong points out that he's leaving and that she'll still be here next week, but that's not the point. I owe it to Jimmy to see him off right.

The whole time we're talking I notice this guy sitting across from me; his buzzed hair, torn jeans and Janis Joplin T-shirt stand out among the normal Korean fashions. He's the only person on the train not staring at his phone, and though he tries not to look at me as I speak, I can tell he understands what I'm saying. Eun-seong and I decide to talk it over more at lunch tomorrow, so I hang up, tilt my head back, and close my eyes. When I open them a moment later, the seat across from me is empty and the guy has appeared in the seat beside me.

"Hello," he says. And before I can respond, "Where are you from?"

"Nowhere," I say. And I wait for the blank stare.

"Ah. I know that place."

"Do you? How's that?"

"I also come from nowhere. What is the name of your nowhere?"

"Sevierville, Tennessee, U.S.A," I tell him. "And your nowhere?"

"Jeolla-do. The town name is the Korean word for 'nowhere'."

This makes me smile. I've always liked messing with people, but it's been a while since anyone's given it back. "Not really, though," I say.

"Okay-okay," he says, still grinning. "Why did you come to Korea?"

"Nowhere got boring," I tell him.

"Ah," he says as he taps a finger to his chest.

"Same." He looks to the metal rack above our seat where I put my guitar case. "Is 'nowhere' the place you learned to play guitar?" I tell him it was. "What kind of music do you play?"

"A bit of everything. Rock, folk, the blues..."

"Yes, I know blues. I am a harmonica player." He looks proud of this statement. "There are not many Korean blues musicians. We should play together."

"Can you play as well as you speak English?"

He sighs and thinks it over, like he's taking the question seriously. "I think about the same."

"Then I'm in."

"Great! I heard you will play a gig tomorrow." For a moment I wonder if I'm being stalked, but then I remember he'd been eavesdropping.

"That's right," I say. "It's in the HBC area, by Itaewon."

"Yes, I know this area."

"Do you know a place called 'Phillies'?"

"I think so," he says. I tell him it's next to Bonnie's Pizza and his eyes light up. "Yes, I know. What time?" I tell him the gig starts at eight-thirty, and before I get a chance to invite him, he declares, "I will come and see you play blues." He pauses as his eyes shoot up and to the left —a look I know well. It's the look we get when the foreign words we need are just beyond the edge of our memory. "I will bring my harmonicas and show my skill."

The transfer music plays and he stands. "This is

my stop. I am happy to meet you," he says, so I tell him my name and ask for his. "Ho-joon," he tells me, and I say goodbye in Korean while he waves with both hands for a few seconds longer than he needs to and disappears through the doors.

● ● ●

I run up the escalator at Sadang, hoping to catch the pigeon man before he leaves. The pigeon man is a street vendor who grills sticks with chicken, green onion and rice cakes and sells two of them for three-thousand won, if you can find him. He appears on my corner randomly and with as much logic as Chinese smog or the speaker trucks that blast out phone numbers loud enough to wake me twenty stories up—*Kong. Ill. Kong. Ku. Pal. Ku. Sa.* . . I have no clue where he sets up when he's not set up here, but I do know that, when the clock strikes ten-thirty, he's gone faster than a new Korean word from my memory.

Ten-ten and no sign of the pigeon man. Looks like its Kimbap Cheonguk, the poor-man's paradise, for dinner tonight. I grab *jaeyook dup-bap* to go and a few beers from the CU at the base of the 32-story tower I call home, buzz myself into the lobby, nod-bow to the guy behind the desk and go check my mail. A card from my grandmother and a flier for a pork restaurant featuring a cute cartoon pig in a chef hat. I stand back from the elevator and wait as it stops at four different floors while a girl with earphone cords coming through her hair, who's either crazy or talking to someone on speakerphone, crowds the door as it opens and tries to push her way on before anyone else can get off. She bolts through the doors on the eighth floor and I ride up to twenty alone. I enter my apartment alone. I eat dinner and shower alone. I think of messaging someone but the trains end in an hour and I'm low on funds anyway, so I watch a movie and drink my beers alone. And later, I lay down to sleep alone in an apartment that is basically a box with a window for the far wall, an apartment where both owner and tenant never got around to putting up curtains, so now the random lights of the city's other boxes shine upon me like the stars I no longer see in the night sky, the stars I have to trust are still there, same as they were before, same as they've always been.

● ● ●

The next day I meet Eun-seong for lunch at a conveyor sushi restaurant near Ganghwamun. A bit out of my price range but she says she can pay and that her father's company will cover it out of his expense account. The perks of dating an executive's daughter. I grab a few of the best plates to get us started.

Eun-seong's firm about me meeting her family, but don't write her off as bossy or controlling. She's actually a sweetheart. Today she's brought me a present—a guitar pic featuring the Kakao bear wildly strumming his own guitar. It's the wrong size for my playing style but she says that's okay, I don't have to use the thing, she just knew it would make me smile. And she's right. That's how sweet she is.

She's sorry she has to bartend that night and won't be able to make my gig. I tell her that's okay. She asks what I plan to do after and I remind her I'm going out with Jimmy. She lets out a sigh and an *aigoo*. She claims to like Jimmy, but he's got an intensity that brings out the wild side in anyone around him and I can tell she's glad he's leaving. She asks if I still plan to stay out all night like I promised. I remind her that I keep my promises.

"Then promise me you'll stop drinking early."

"That promise would contradict the other promise."

"You just don't want to meet my parents." She lets a choice plate of salmon sushi pass and instead grabs grilled corn.

"You're right," I tell her. "I've never denied that. I'm not looking to get married any time soon."

"I told you they don't expect that." She makes herself a second cup of green tea while I grab more tuna. "They just want to meet you. They've never met a foreigner. So please be in a good condition."

I tell her I'll try my best, but the words come out as more of a hope than a promise. She wants to meet at noon, which should give me at least a little time to sleep and pull myself together. I'll look tired, but it's not every day your best friend moves away. If her parents can't understand that, I doubt we'd get along anyway.

• • •

I limit myself to one beer before a gig. Okay, maybe two or three. But I always hit the brakes if I start feeling buzzed. Not very "rock star", I know, but when you play acoustic there's no drumbeat to keep you in time, no feedback to cover your mistakes. You've got to stay on your toes. That's why I never eat too much before a gig either. It weighs you down.

That being said, Jimmy's last night is a special occasion, so I agree to meet him and a few of our old *hagwon* co-workers at Magpie for beer and pizza around six, and by the time we head to Phillies at seven-thirty, I can't tell if I'm buzzed or stuffed or a combination of both. The walk does me good though, and I'm feeling light on my feet again when I see Hojoon standing up on the patio, talking to Seong-eun.

"You didn't tell me you played with a violin," Hojoon says while Seong-eun comes around to give me and the rest of the crew a hug. Inside, an opener I've never met is covering Oasis too quietly to steal the dinner crowd's attention away from their burgers and beers and conversations.

"Not enough time," I tell him.

"Violin and harmonica do not go together. It's not

common." That's when I feel Jimmy's hand on my shoulder.

"All the more reason to give it a go," Jimmy says. He's shaved his hair into a mohawk since I've last seen him and is decked out in leather and chains.

"We've got a few bluesy songs that don't feel right with the violin," Seong-eun tells him. "They'd be perfect for harmonica."

My thoughts exactly.

Ho-joon wants to play on those songs tonight, no practice ahead of time, which shouldn't be a problem as long as he knows the blues. My father used to say that every twelve bars of the blues is like being born, dying, and being born again. Every song—like every player, every life—builds its own story from that same pattern, and that story can be about anything, not just sadness, though there's always some sense of sadness when dying's involved. Some people think that pattern makes all blues sound the same, and in the hands of players with no story to tell, they're right. But it's also what makes the blues one of the only kinds of music where you can meet a bunch of strangers, shout out a key, and jam all night without anyone hitting a wrong note.

Birth, death, and rebirth, over and over again. And if you do it enough times, you learn how to make it your own. That's the blues.

Ho-joon and I walk down the side street to where it's quiet while everyone else heads to the bar. I take out my guitar and run through both songs with him once, showing him where I think a harmonica solo would fit. He nods at everything I say, bobs his head when I play like he's trying to feel what I've got, trying to let it take him over, trying to imagine what it could become. But he doesn't take out any harmonicas, doesn't play along. I ask him if he wants to and he just shakes his head and tells me he will be okay.

We head back to the bar, and now it's Seong-eun's turn to drag me away, down the same side street, so we can talk.

"Why didn't you tell me you're meeting your girl-friend's parents?"

"I just found out last night."

"No time to run away, huh?" Seong-eun's feelings for my girlfriend both feed and feed off of Eun-seong's feelings for her. My girlfriend, who learned English from academies and Western culture from episodes of Friends, is a bit jealous and distrustful of my bandmate, who learned both those things by spending nearly half her life in the United States. This jealousy and distrust make my bandmate concerned, so she coaches me on dating Korean women. Her advice works until my girlfriend figures out its source, which creates more jealousy and distrust, which leads to more concern. And the cycle continues, pushing my two worlds apart.

"It's not like that."

"Don't do it. You're not ready. And you'll be in no

shape for it tomorrow."

"I know. But she really wants me to. And I am a bit curious. It's not like I ever get invited to your parents' place."

Seong-eun laughs. "I bet she'd love that. You know she messaged me last night. Wants me to look out for you, make sure you don't get too drunk. As if I could slow you or Jimmy down."

"You slow us down without trying."

"She's going to blame me if you're in rough shape tomorrow."

"She'll blame Jimmy."

"Jimmy will be gone."

"Oh yeah." I say it with a smirk that fades. Seong-eun's expression changes too. I ask her what I should do.

"Call her and tell her you're not ready. At least it's honest."

"I don't know."

She comes up to me and hugs me. We hug to say hello and goodbye, but this one feels different, almost sympathetic. "It's okay," she says in my ear. "You don't have to be perfect all the time. She'll understand."

"She'll be pissed."

She pulls away. "Not if you say it right."

"I'll be fine. Stop worrying."

Seong-eun rolls her eyes, sighs, and heads back to the bar.

● ● ●

Jimmy's last night and the crowd it provides make for one hell of a gig. Everyone's there to see Jimmy and Jimmy's there to see me. This means that, for the time Seong-eun and I are on stage, we've got the crowd's attention, the way I like it. I don't do background music, and neither does she. We want to be heard.

We run through a few covers and a few originals until we reach the point where Seong-eun takes a break for a few songs and I go solo. Like always, the crowd is bummed to see her go, but she'll be back for the last few songs. I cover The Clash because I know it will get Jimmy, and by extension everyone else, dancing and singing along. Now it's time for one of my original blues songs, one of Jimmy's favorites, and so I call Ho-joon up to the stage. The crowd cheers. He gives a little wave, but as the silence sets in I can tell this man I barely know is nervous.

Ho-joon, says *"Anyeonghaseyo"* into Seong-eun's vocal mic and a few people cheer. He goes over to the PA and turns his mic down. In a place this small, I didn't expect him to even use a mic, but here he is, holding the harmonica up to it and playing basic notes, nothing fancy at all, like he's tuning it, even though harmonicas don't work that way. Just when I think he's going to impress me with something showy he

85

stops and looks at me to start the song.

And here we go.

I start the song the way I always do, by explaining it's about guys using language exchange programs to hit on Korean girls back before the days of Tinder. Jimmy cheers. Of all my songs, this is his favorite, and I start to think I should have asked Jimmy to be nice if Ho-joon bombs. Jimmy's never shy about booing someone for messing up something he likes. I play the intro and see Ho-joon begin to sway to the rhythm. The smile that never seemed to leave his face is gone as I sing the first verse:

Teach me "hello", teach me "goodbye"
Teach me "thank you" and teach me "nice try"
Teach me "hell yes", teach me "oh no"
Teach me what I should say at your door
Teach me what can't be found in a dictionary
Oh girl, teach me what your words mean

Next is a short instrumental break before the second verse, a place I told Ho-joon he could play a short warm-up if he wanted. He puts his harmonica to his lips and plays one long, solid note.

Then he goes crazy.

Ho-joon starts jumping around scales like a pro, milking each note, and the crowd starts to cheer as I keep the rhythm going and going far longer than I'd planned because I don't know when, or if, this guy's going to stop. Remember, this is just a break—not the main soloing part for the song. I'm not sure if he forgot or doesn't care. He's too busy blowing everyone away to even consider stopping. And no one wants him to stop. Not me. Not Jimmy, whose eyes and mouth are as wide open as they get. Not Seong-eun, who's studying him like he's giving a lecture. Everyone's cheering this guy on to keep going. So he does. He keeps going, well past the point where he should have passed out from lack of air.

When he finally stops, his face is red and he's breathing like he just swam up from the bottom of the sea, but then I finish the next verse, and it's time for the real solo to begin.

● ● ●

After that, Ho-joon is a member of our crew for the night. Jimmy insists he stick around, and since it's Jimmy's party, not even a stranger can turn him down.

If Eun-seong came out with us more often, she would know that. If she came out with us more often, she wouldn't be asking me to turn him down. And if she came out more often, she wouldn't always end up a topic of conversation.

But it's not her fault. Like most unmarried Korean girls, she still lives with her parents. And though I'm sworn to secrecy because she's embarrassed about it, she misses out on these nights because she has a curfew.

So when my friends ask me about her, I change the subject. But my friends know me. After a few more drinks, when my own situation seems more important, they'll be asking again.

● ● ●

"Drink up, mate," Jimmy yells from the pool table to Ho-joon at the bar. It's the prime partying time of the night and we're one of the only groups of people in an otherwise dead joint on Hooker Hill. As the name implies, the only people that come to this part of Itaewon are guys looking to buy hookers. But Jimmy wants a pool game and this place has three tables. So here we are.

Ho-joon is pretty drunk after a round of shots—not falling-down, making-no-sense drunk, but can't-stop-smiling, forgetting-his-English drunk—so he talks to Seong-eun in Korean most of the time. Jimmy's kicking my ass at pool yet again when the two of them come over with another round of shots and set them down at the table. I've been trying to avoid shots all night, and now all eyes are on me.

"Don't you say it," Jimmy says. "Don't say you can't." We take the shot together. "Oh, he did it!" Jimmy screams, pointing at me like I'm caught. "I'm going to message your bird right now!"

Ho-joon asks Seong-eun, in Korean, what Jimmy's

talking about, and I can pick up just enough to know Seong-eun's filling him in. Ho-joon's eyes light up.

"Subway," he says, holding his hand to his head like it's a phone. The other day, his eavesdropping. I nod and he and Seong-eun go back to talking. I don't care to listen and go back to shooting pool. God knows what he overheard me saying on the subway the other day.

Later Ho-joon holds up a cigarette and motions for me to follow him outside. I shake my head and tell him I quit, but he's not having it. He practically pushes me out the door with him, and it doesn't take long for me to learn why.

"Seong-eun," he says. I can tell he's struggling for the words. He starts in Korean but stops himself. "I want to date."

I laugh a little, put my hand on his shoulder and tell him, "*Aniyo. Namja chingu isseoyo.*"

"No," he says.

"Yes she does."

"Aniya," he says, putting his hands up to form an X.

"Yes she does," I insist. "She has forever."

He types something into his phone and I read the translation over his shoulder: "I broke up." I know the "I" is supposed to be "she" but I don't believe it.

"What?" I say. "No way. When?"

"Three days before."

For a moment I'm not sure what to believe. Seong-eun never said a word about it to me, and yet she tells this stranger she just met? I decide not to believe him. Who knows what kind of guy this stranger is, or what kind of game he might be running? I decide I need to run this by Seong-eun before I decide what's what.

I go to move past Ho-joon and he stops me. "Date, okay?" he asks.

"No," I tell him. "It's too soon."

He grins and starts pretending to play basketball. He dribbles his invisible ball, shoots, and jumps up to catch it. "Rebound?" I ask. He shakes his head. God knows how he picked up that term. "No," I say again. "Too soon."

He nods politely. "Ok, I understand," he says. And we walk back up together.

● ● ●

Later, when pool gets boring, Jimmy and Ho-joon take an interest in the girl working behind the bar. That's when I maneuver Seong-eun out of earshot.

"Did you and Jae-won break up?"

"Ho-joon told you already? That guy wastes no time."

"Why didn't you tell me?"

"You think your girlfriend doesn't like us playing together now? Imagine what she'd say if she knew I was single."

She's got me there. I take a breath and ask her

what happened.

"I just realized I didn't want to spend the rest of my life with him. He's a great guy, and I hope we stay friends, but our parents set us up."

I've never known this detail; I ask her to explain.

"Well, it's not like I only dated him for that reason. They knew I didn't want to date a Korean guy, but they pushed us into a date, and I liked him. I'd just got back to Korea and he was different. It felt right then."

"But not anymore?"

She's getting a bit choked up. "I wish I could say he cheated on me or something, but that's not true. I just can't picture the rest of my life with him. I finally worked up the courage to tell him, and he said if that were true, there was no reason going on. Which I guess is also true."

"Why now? What changed your mind?"

"You." I must have looked shocked because she added, "no, no. Not like that. Don't worry. It's just that after I answered your ad to play, I started to meet so many Westerners, like you and Jimmy and the girls at the bar, and it started to remind me of the States, of everything else out there, how people can just pick up and leave and do whatever they want with their life. And if I marry him, I'll be stuck in Seoul forever."

Funny, I thought, to think of Seoul as a place to be "stuck". That word fit my hometown just fine, Ho-joon's too, but not here, not this mega-city.

But I guess anywhere can feel like nowhere if you stay there long enough.

Seong-eun hasn't really cried, but she pulls herself together anyway. "Thank you for listening," she says, just like one of my students after a presentation. She hears it herself and it makes us both giggle. "I feel better now."

"After talking or after breaking up?"

"Both." She stares into my eyes. We've looked each other in the eye countless times—as friends, as musicians telling each other how to play—but this time feels different. A lot feels different.

Then Seong-eun, my friend who is also a girl, kisses me on the cheek, stands up, and walks over to our friends at the bar. I follow, and the night goes on.

● ● ●

Ho-joon's in it for the long haul, he says. Until the first train starts running. And that's when I decide: so am I. I tell Jimmy that I'll follow him to the ends of the Earth if that's what he wants from me, and if Eun-seong wants to break up over it, then that's her decision. My reward— round of cheers and applause and free drinks at the next bar. But I don't feel like I've won, or they've won, or Eun-seong's lost. It's not that kind of decision. I've just bought the night on credit. I'll find out the cost tomorrow.

• • •

We hit up Thunderhorse for a punk show while Jimmy's trendier friends head to some club in Hongdae. After that it's shots and beers at Sam Ryan's and late-night gyros from that street vendor in front of the English bookstore no one goes to. Ho-joon sticks close to Seong-eun at first, but I can tell he's sobered up a bit because his English abilities return and he's talking to Jimmy about his plans back in England and a distant relative who works in the K-pop industry and all the ways our guitar, violin and harmonica act could change the future of Korean music. It's all drunk talk, but I let myself get carried into the fantasy. It's nice to feel the future of anything could be in your hands.

We hit up a basement bar I've never been to before, have long, deep discussions that won't change anything. When we come out the sun is up. The trains and buses have started running again. Jimmy lives south of the city and I offer to buy him a KTX ticket so he doesn't have to take the subway for two hours. I just hope he doesn't wake up in Busan.

Seong-eun's stop is on the way to Seoul station. She tears up a little when it's her turn to say goodbye, closes her eyes as she hugs him. When she opens her eyes, she's looking at me. She waves goodbye as the doors close and the train moves on, and then it's just the three of us.

I buy Jimmy a train ticket at the station and we

walk to the outer area where the escalators take you down to the platforms. Ho-joon says he has to go to the bathroom, that he might be sick and might not be back before Jimmy's train leaves, so he says goodbye and asks me to wait for him. Now it's just me and Jimmy.

I see Jimmy off the way we've both seen off other friends over the years. They say it gets easier, and that's true for those who come here after you, those who only stay a short time, those you didn't really get to know.

But this is Jimmy.

We hug, wish each other luck, promise to stay in touch, run through the other clichés, keep smiles on our faces and tears from our eyes. One last hug and he heads down the escalator. I go the opposite way, up those steps leading up to nowhere, and have a seat next to my guitar. I've almost forgotten about Ho-joon when he comes up to me.

"He's gone?" Ho-joon asks. I nod. "But you will see him again." This isn't a question, like it is in my own head. Ho-joon has no doubt I will see Jimmy again.

We walk back into the station. When I start to head toward the subway, Ho-joon stops me, tells me the bus is faster. For the first time all night, he looks exhausted, like he can't wait to get home.

"I know," I tell him. "But I didn't know that back when I first got here, back when Jimmy and I first

94

met." I can tell he's not sure why this matters, but I'm too tired to explain it. "Go ahead and take the bus. I'll message you this week and we'll meet up."

"I can join you on the subway," he offers.

"Jimmy and I used to take the subway home together before he moved. I think I'd like to take it alone this time."

"Why?"

"In his honor. For old time's sake. I don't know."

He thinks about this for a minute, like maybe he didn't understand my words.

Then I see something click.

"The blues?" he asks, and in that moment I want to take my guitar out of its case, set up in the center of Seoul station and play for hours, play for all the other late-night partiers, for the families with their kids, for the *ajummas* and the *ajusshis*, for the foreigners from all the ends of the Earth, for all the Jimmys and the Ho-joons and the Eun-seongs and the Seong-euns and anyone else who knows what it is to say goodbye to a night and hello to a new day.

But it's time to say goodbye to the night. And I can't change that.

"Yes," I tell him.

The blues.

Matthew Grolemund has lived in South Korea for the past five years. During that time, he has had numerous experiences that served as inspiration for "Playing the Blues in Seoul," such as marrying into a Korean family, learning modest levels of Korean, and performing at several musical gigs in Seoul. He holds an M.F.A. in Creative Writing from Wichita State University in the United States and has published stories in literary journals such as *Redivider, The Ampersand Review, Permafrost, Jelly Bucket, Compose,* and elsewhere. He currently teaches at Soonchunhyang University in Asan and is completing his first novel. You can find him playing acoustic gigs in Seoul under the name Matty Grols, on twitter @magrols and you can listen to his original music at 99bpm.bandcamp.com.

> Gord Sellar

Sojourn

"When he leaned forward again and glanced at the form, he realized she was pointing at the checkboxes beside the questions, Are you a genetic deviant? Have you ever exhibited genetic deviant traits? Do you have family members who are genetic deviants? The checkboxes were all unmarked."

To anyone else, the little rice field would have looked out of place, a patch of viridian dropped onto the edge of a grungy neighborhood, but to Trevor it was a defiant miracle. As he walked past it to work every day, it sang—not to him, not to anyone, but its song shimmered into Trevor's muscles all the same, as if the microbial choirs teeming in the muck were calling out to him on purpose.

For Trevor, the field shone, as luminous as the midsummer sun above. Its simultaneous exhalations of carbon dioxide, methane, and oxygen were as sensuous as a warm bath, the rippling aggregate consciousness of the microbial stew as colorful as any masterpiece on a museum wall. In the time it took him to walk to work, enormous, microscopic worlds merged and separated, empires of unconscious memory rising and falling and rising again.

And Trevor was unfailingly grateful for it, for the spectacle eclipsed the smog, the snarling of angry cars a few blocks away, the blasting of a speaker over the doors of little shops near campus. Those all lost out to the rich, unfathomable harmony of the rice field's soundless song, and for Trevor it was a kind of solace. He actually felt sad for the rest of the world: the mundanes, of course, but even the other gifted he knew, because like the mundanes, none of them—not the unbreakables or the unmoveables, neither the herculeans nor the psions—had even seen the world the way he did. The only people who understood what he perceived were microbiologists, and their grasp was ultimately a little shallow, like talking to people who knew the gist of a book but had only seen the movie. Even when he was careful to not let on too much, they inevitably got a funny look on their faces and said, *How do you know so much about this stuff?*

The irony was how little they knew, how much they were in the dark about, stumbling around blindfolded. Trevor felt things their theories didn't encompass, sensed processes the microbiologists never seemed to imagine or leave room for among their calculations. And as he did every day, Trevor felt sad for the poverty of all those around him who, like those microbiologists, were clueless about the gorgeous, cataclysmic diversity that saturated the world around them.

A horn honked loudly. Trevor turned and saw a minibus pulling up behind him. The driver, a familiar older man, waved to Trevor, who dutifully stepped to the edge of the road to let it pass. There were kids to be delivered to the Language Center after all, and the bus was on a tight schedule.

But then, so am I, Trevor thought, quickening his pace.

• • •

After Soo-jin's pencil box crashed back down to her desk, it took a moment for her to realize what had happened.

She was sitting alone in the classroom, and Trevor Teacher was standing in the doorway, his eyes wide. He glanced over his shoulder, and Soo-jin glanced down at her pencil box—now lying open, a couple of her pencils having spilled out—before she looked at him again.

She met his eyes for a second, just to try and judge whether he'd seen—whether he'd understood what he'd seen. Soo-jin knew that people sometimes rationalized things, or chose to ignore what they couldn't explain away. But Trevor Teacher *had* seen, she realized; he was trying to be discreet about it, but he *knew*.

Still, as her classmates began filtering into the room, chattering with one another, he said nothing. She could see him looking at her, clearly nervous, but trying to hide it as he began teaching the class.

Soo-jin silently contracted into herself, and suddenly felt the rest of the world recede, as if it were a million miles away, and she were safe at some hidden place deep within her own body. After changing schools so many times, after so many warnings from her mother and father, she had done it again. Guilt and shame seeped out of her muscles and bones, familiar and sour. She hadn't done it on purpose—hadn't dared to make anything float in the air for years. It was just that sometime . . . Sometimes it happened on its own, around her.

She had seen enough on TV, read enough of her mom's books, to know it was probably stress. The strain of always hiding her powers, of course, but even just all the studying, the pressure to get into a good middle school, the way girls in her class were starting to turn mean or bossy or cold to her, the growing pains she felt in her limbs. She wanted to stand, to stretch her legs. She wanted to sleep. But most of all, she yearned to float herself into the air. She knew she mustn't—but to stretch out, in the warm afternoon sun and soar . . .

That's a stupid daydream, Soo-jin told herself. *You're not even supposed to think about that.* She focused back on the textbook, as Trevor Teacher read some of the text, and asked students to suggest words that could fit into the blanks of the book. She stared at her pencil box, her eyes tracing the crack in its side that must have appeared when it had slammed against the desk earlier.

"Anyone? What is it?" Trevor Teacher asked. "Soo-jin?"

"Pencil box!" she blurted out, without thinking, and immediately blushed.

Trevor Teacher was thrown off by that. "Uh . . . sure. 'Do you have a pencil box in your bag, Soo-jin?'" he asked, reading out the practice sentence from the book.

She looked down at her desk, muttering, "Yes."

Students, she knew, smelled distraction and anxiety the way dogs sensed fear; the whole class looked at her, eyebrows raised, and Mi-na, the girl who sat beside her, suddenly shouted, "Look!"

Soo-jin gasped, panicking as she glanced up into the air above her desk. *Nonononono*, she thought, but when she glanced back down again, she saw her pencil case not floating after all, but innocently sitting on the desktop next to her textbook.

"It's on her desk!" Mi-na half-shouted, turning to beam at Trevor Teacher as the other kids laughed. Soo-jin blushed.

He awkwardly congratulated Mi-na on her percep-tiveness: "Right, she should say, 'No, I don't have a pencil box in my bag'. Everybody?"

Soo-jin stared at Mi-na out of the corner of her eye as everyone repeated the sentence. She was pretty, tall, good at English, and popular—everything Soo-jin wasn't. Not that she was ugly, but she just wasn't as noticeable. Suddenly, like a fever, her envy rose: why couldn't Mi-na have been the one born with some-thing to hide, to have to worry about others' searching eyes?

"Right," Trevor Teacher replied, and Soo-jin could see how eager he was to change the subject. She searched his face, worried. Wasn't it different where he came from? Weren't "deviants" called "gifted" there? Her mom had said they weren't taken away by the police, or put in special schools, or forced to do anything they didn't want except register with the gov-ernment. She'd thought in Canada it was okay to be different. She'd seen a documentary one night on TV, about deviants in other countries; about how the par-ents of deviant kids in Canada had fought, so they would be called "gifted" instead, and she'd longed to live there, asked her parents to move there. When her parents had gone silent and her mom had started weeping, she'd dropped it; but she'd never forgotten about it.

If all that was true, then what was Trevor Teacher's problem?

The class dragged on that day, a little eternity between each tick of the clock, until finally it was time for everyone to run for their buses and move on to their next *hagwon*. Everyone packed up their pencil boxes and textbooks frantically, rushing out while Soo-jin hung back, sitting with her book open as if working out a question for Trevor Teacher.

As soon as it was just the two of them left in the room, Trevor Teacher looked over to her and said awkwardly, "Are you okay, Soo-jin?"

She took her notebook over to him and asked, "Is this sentence right?" She handed it over, her finger pointing at the line she'd scribbled in pencil: *Please, Trevor Teacher, don't tell . . . keep it secret, please!*

He looked up from the notebook, and nodded. "But here's a better way to write it . . ." And with a red pen, he crossed out her words before scribbling, I didn't see anything, Soo-jin. Don't worry. Does your mother know? He pointed at the sentence, and said, "See?"

Soo-jin nodded. He wrote, *YOU NEED TO BE MORE CAREFUL!*

She nodded again. With a smile he said, "Go catch your bus, kiddo."

Soo-jin hurried out, longing to simply hop over the atrium balcony railing and float down to the ground floor; that way, she'd have beaten them all downstairs. She *knew* she could have; but instead she simply hurried over to the stairs, making sure—for dramatic effect—to stumble a little as she went.

After all, nobody ever suspected a plain-faced, awkward girl who stumbled on the stairs of being anything but what she seemed.

● ● ●

Out in the hallway, a moment later, Trevor was locking up when another teacher on staff strode up to him. It was Cam, a rheumy-eyed slacker from Vancouver who reeked faintly of cigarette smoke and booze as usual.

"You goin' for dinner, bro?" Cam asked.

"Yeah, I think so," Trevor said.

"I need to eat before my fuckin' seven o'clock class. Whaddaya say, we go get some *kimchi bokkeumbap* or something?"

Two weeks into term, the guy was still cursing about evening class he'd agreed to teach. It was all about the overtime pay, with Cam, and the late class was easy; advanced level free-talking meant no prep and one less beginner class to teach in the afternoon.

"How's that class going, anyway?" Trevor asked as he locked his classroom door, wrinkling his nose. Cam must have had a late night the day before, because he hadn't showered that day at all—his dermal microbiota was crawling, louder and more raucous than Trevor had seen on anyone in days. There was a sourness in his breath, too, unfamiliar and alarming to

Trevor. In the hopes of steering Cam away from his bitchfest, he asked Cam, "You said the students were pretty good, right?"

"Aw, not bad, you know . . . I don't have to actually fuckin' do squat," he said, whispering the curse word as a crowd of elementary schoolers scampered past them down the hall. "I mean, besides sit and shoot the shit. And you know Hye-gyeong?"

Trevor nodded; he knew Hye-gyeong. Everyone at the Language Center knew Hye-gyeong.

Cam grinned. "She's in that class. Smokin' . . . she's on the hunt, too. Freaks out all the college boys in the class. Funniest shit you ever saw. . ."

"Ha," Trevor said, smiling awkwardly back at his coworker. As much as he resented the assumptions people made about foreign English teachers, people like Cam reminded him that the stereotype existed for a reason. As he eyed his co-worker, Trevor wondered just what he'd fled all the way to Korea to avoid: collection agencies calling about overdue student loans? A fucked-up family? A nightmare breakup? Most of the expats he knew had come fleeing something, and with the guys it was usually the last one. Whatever the case, practically every expat he knew in Korea had, on some level, come here to escape something back home.

Even me, he thought to himself sarcastically. He then noticed Director Kim coming down the hall, looking the same as usual in her black pencil skirt and white blouse, with an annoyed look on her bespecta-cled face and a clipboard clutched to her chest. She appeared to be staring straight at him and Cam.

"Dude," Trevor whispered, "Boss is coming. Did you smoke in class again?"

"Fuck, no," Cam mumbled, his tone a weird mix of detachment and resentment. Then, louder, "Dude, I'm not stupid." As if lighting up a cigarette in a kids' class a second time somehow constituted the basic standard for stupidity.

But as Director Kim reached them, she turned to Cam and said, "Excuse me, Cam."

He turned to her, half-bowing, and said, "Yes?"

"Excuse me," she said again. When he stared at her blankly, she added, "I need to talk to Trevor here. Alone."

"Oooh, alright," Cam said, obviously relieved as he glanced toward Trevor. "Have a nice night, *Wonjang-nim!*"

For his part, Trevor was fighting the urge to correct her: *Excuse us*, he kept thinking. *He'd have left if you'd said, "Please excuse us."* It was the English teacher's burden, that urge to correct everyone's im-perfect speech all the time.

She ignored Cam's parting comment, and turned to look up at Trevor with an expression even more serious than usual. "Trevor," she began, pushing her glasses up her nose with one finger.

"Yes, *Wonjang-nim?*" he asked, respectfully.

She smiled now—the kind of feral smile that made Trevor's blood cold. He eyed the clipboard, bracing himself for the world to fall down all around him like a pallet of bricks dropped out of an airplane.

As she flipped the clipboard to show it to Trevor, his blood ran cold. On some level he'd been waiting for this moment for months, ever since he'd first gotten to Korea. Which grainy newspaper photograph would it be? The one where he and the Prairie Riders had destroyed White Peter's bioweapon shed in Regina, and Wildfire's boyfriend had leaked their identities to the press? The one where they'd refused to cooperate with the national military, and a referendum had been called on whether "gifted" people should be allowed to live in Calgary? Or maybe the one that the newspapers had published when the RCMP had issued warrants for their arrest, after their showdown with the government's construction crews on the day the CBC studios in Edmonton had been set to be demolished?

But when she flipped the clipboard to face him, he saw only an official-looking form. No lurid article, no newspaper pictures. She scowled up at him, and asked, "Did you fill this out honestly?"

Trevor fought his instinct to sigh from relief, and leaned forward—she was a short woman—to discover that it was the application form he'd filled out and mailed from Calgary, a month before taking this job and flying to Korea. It felt like so long ago, though it'd only been a year and a half.

He straightened his back and nodded his head. "Of course, *Wonjang-nim*," he said.

But she just smiled a little more harshly and said, "Here?" When he leaned forward again and glanced at the form, he realized she was pointing at the checkboxes beside the questions, Are you a genetic deviant? Have you ever exhibited genetic deviant traits? Do you have family members who are genetic deviants? The checkboxes were all unmarked.

He straightened up, suddenly worried. *But how . . . .?*

"We have hidden cameras in all the classrooms. To protect the children . . ."

Trevor winced; he understood what Cam had hinted darkly at, a few weeks before, while explaining how Australian Rod had achieved the near-Olympian feat of getting himself fired from the easiest job on Earth.

"And I'm sure you know about the Korean laws regarding deviants. It's in the Ministry of Immigration's pamphlet."

Trevor nodded, though he wanted more than anything to snarl at her: *Don't use that word.* But instead, he just nodded and said, "Yes, *Wonjang-nim*, but. . . what is this about?" Playing dumb; it was worth a shot.

"I saw you. . . with Soo-jin. And the pencil box."

Trevor inhaled, looking into her squinting eyes.

"I don't know what you mean," he tried, hoping she might back down.

"I saw you make her pencil box float . . ."

"No I didn't!" Trevor blurted out without thinking. "That wasn't me, that was . . ." he began, before catching himself.

Director Kim looked confused for a moment, and with a sinking feeling he realized why: she hadn't imagined for an instant that it had been Soo-jin who'd done it. She'd assumed *he* had to be the deviant, that it had to be the foreigner in the room. Trevor scrambled, terrified that he might get deported, that Soo-jin would be in trouble.

"I . . . I . . ." he muttered, searching Director Kim's face as realization dawned in her eyes. And then she understood.

She half-shouted, "Why didn't you come and tell me? You should have come to me immediately."

Then Trevor heard them: sirens, in the distance.

He turned toward the sound for a moment, and said, "What have you done?"

"I just followed the law," she said. "I know you don't understand our culture but this isn't Canada. Here, we . . ."

Frustration and anger welled up in him, and without even pausing to consider what he was doing, Trevor focused his mind on her gut bacteria and told them what to do. When she cried out a moment later, her clipboard clattering to her feet, Trevor grabbed her arm and gently eased her to the ground as he said, a little mechanically, "Are you okay? I'll go get help."

"What did you . . .?" Director Kim began, before

her sentence snapped into a wordless howl of discomfort.

But by then, Trevor was already running for the stairs.

• • •

It was loud on the minibus, with the girls shouting at one another about whether some rumor about Teacher Cam was true, and a pair of oversized, goonish boys staging a wrestling match in the back seat.

Yet just as Soo-jin was about to board the bus, she picked out the sound of distant sirens approaching. She stopped on the first step and glanced around, curious. One of the other girls, a younger, mousy bookworm perched in the front seat, noticed her expression. "What is it?" asked the girl, leaning forward.

Soo-jin didn't answer. Instead she just stood still, glancing around the parking lot. All the other buses had left already; only hers remained.

"Get on, kid," the driver snapped in brusque Korean. "You made us wait too long already, and now we're running late! C'mon . . ." Despite his words, he seemed in no particular hurry. He even turned his head toward the little one-lane paved road that led round the edge of campus to the Language Center, not bothering to close the minibus door.

Soo-jin muttered an apology, and climbed another step up into the bus when she heard someone call out her name from behind her. She turned and saw Trevor Teacher on the front steps of the Language Center, sprinting for the bus and shouting to her. Sweat gleamed on his forehead and soaked through his shirt. His eyes were wide, so wide they scared her, as the door snapped shut and the driver began backing the minibus toward the middle of the parking lot.

"Get off the bus, Soo-jin," Trevor Teacher shouted in English, his voice clearly audible even from far away. Soo-jin stood very still, baffled and staring.

The driver stopped the bus. He turned to stare at the white man approaching them, though he obviously couldn't understand what the man was yelling.

"What the hell?" he muttered before turning to Soo-jin. "Sit down. Let's go," He continued backing the bus out again, even before Soo-jin could take a step—not that she was about to. She was too transfixed by the scene of her English teacher, who seemed to have gone completely insane. As soon as he caught up to the bus, he began pounding on the door and shouting.

"Crazy foreigner," the bus driver muttered, and the door opened with a hiss. "Hey! What the hell?" he shouted at Trevor in Korean.

But Trevor ignored him, his panicked eyes still on Soo-jin. He was talking too fast, but she understood that he wanted her to get off the bus immediately. She heard the sirens again, much closer now, though she saw nothing when she glanced at the side road, nothing but the eyes of all the other kids on the bus, all fixed on her.

Then, her guts sank in an instant as she realized why her teacher was here, beating on the side of the bus and shouting at her. She realized that they were coming for her.

"Why?" she cried out in Korean. "How?"

"Not me!" he shouted in English, and over his shoulder, Soo-jin glimpsed a figure exiting the front doors of the Language Center. It was an older woman in office clothes, struggling against what looked like terrible pain in her guts. Wasn't that Mrs. Kim, the terrifying, much-maligned *wonjang-nim* of the Language Center? Just before she doubled over and fell to her knees with a cry, Mrs. Kim shouted something. Her words were lost, however, in the cacophony of all the other kids on the bus shouting, of the bus driver cursing at Trevor, of Trevor shouting for Soo-jin to get off the bus.

Soo-jin turned and, focusing her mind, willed the door to open. It was stubborn, but after a moment the mechanism jolted hard and the door was suddenly open. Then Soo-jin leaped down the stairs, using her mental powers to soften her landing on the concrete.

"Teacher! Where? She asked, too panicked to bother with grammar.

"I dunno!" He turned his head to the access road as a police van roared up, sirens blaring, pouring out cops armed with net guns and who-knew-what-else.

Soo-jin hoped he might have an idea, but he just closed his eyes.

"Teacher!" she shouted again, but his eyes remained closed. Frantically, she turned once more toward the fleet of police cars. The cops were swarming out of them, and into the parking lot with strange-looking weapons in their hands. They weren't guns, but handheld devices with little radio-frequency dishes on them. A drone soared in over the police van toward the bus. She'd seen the drone before, in a movie, and the radio-dish weapons too.

But then, beyond them—out past the road, above the nearby rice field—Soo-jin saw something she'd never seen before, and couldn't understand. It was some kind of translucent cloud, like mist pouring up into the air, thickening as she watched. The police hadn't noticed it yet, but the kids on the bus had, and they were howling with terror and excitement. The cloud seemed to coalesce, its density concentrating for a moment, before it poured down toward the vans and cars and all of the cops.

Soo-jin turned to face Trevor again: his eyes were still closed, and he was clearly straining.

Whatever it was, that cloud was under his control.

Then he opened his eyes, gasping for air. He glanced around, searching for something—somewhere to run.

"Teacher, teacher! Where?" she asked again.

The police officers began coughing and sneezing,

some of them driven mad by a sudden outbreak of hives and itching. Some of them, but not all. Just as Trevor Teacher was about to speak, a voice amplified by a megaphone filled the air, drowning out everything else with its demand in deafening Korean syllables: "Where is the deviant?"

Trevor Teacher didn't seem to understand the cops. He ignored the shouting and just muttered a useless answer to her question: "I don't know." He glanced around again. "I'm thinking! I . . ."

"No." She grabbed his forearm firmly. Trevor Teacher was jolted out of his panic, and looked at her now with clear, surprised eyes. Soo-jin said, "No. I . . ."

Then, with a sudden surge of Soo-jin's will, the two of them were thrown into the air—and they did not fall. Hanging onto his arm, Soo-jin shouted again, "Where, Teacher?"

Trevor found himself about to prompt her to use a full sentence, but then he glanced down at the ground and laughed, a little giddy and obviously astonished, before looking back up toward Soo-jin in wonder. With the sky behind her, floating beside him, a dozen feet up, she was smiling as he'd never before seen her do. He wanted to cry out, to tell her he'd never flown before, never known anyone "gifted" who was so strong at such a young age, but he saw the cops were raising their radio-dish weapons toward them, so instead just shouted: "Up! Faster!"

They shot straight up into the blue sky, and soared over the rice field, still hurtling upward without stopping, ignoring the voices and the flashing police-car lights below, and the cops with their dish-guns, and all the kids and teachers who'd poured out from the building. Soo-jin glanced down at the crowd they were leaving behind. The kids were all pointing and shouting, crowded around the horrified-looking bus driver. The cops were crouched, their weapons and megaphones useless now, their drone unable to catch up to Trevor and little Soo-jin. They chattered to one another as the megaphone voice continued its pointless, now-incomprehensible yelling.

As they plummeted upward, Trevor saw that a couple of English teachers had gathered on a balcony of the Language Center, one holding up his smart phone and filming the miracle of their flight, while another—was it Teacher Cam?—jumped up and down, cheering. The figures were just barely distinguishable from one another, but they were already so far away that their faces were indistinct. This, Trevor realized, was the only goodbye he'd have with them. He didn't mind, though.

Soo-jin, too, was looking down, back at the mist-clouded chaos they were leaving behind. Everyone's eyes were on her, but for the first time in her life, she no longer cared who stared at her, or gaped, or thought she was weird. She didn't care because she was finally being herself.

It was wonderful, and Trevor Teacher clearly thought so too: he whooped with glee, and shouted, "This is amazing, Soo-jin! Amazing! You're powerful, kid!"

She could feel that power, coursing through her. How long had she kept it pent up inside her, caged like an animal that ought to have been set free? She'd tried so hard to be like them, these kids who were normal. She'd envied them and longed to be the same as them, but now, she knew, she wasn't and couldn't be—and no longer wanted it, either. With the wind in her hair, buffeting her smiling face, and the pull of gravity fainter already as she soared toward the city, she felt absolutely amazing.

Trevor Teacher watched her exulting in her powers, and memories flooded through him. He'd known what it was like to hide his gifts, to want to fit in, to be like everyone else. He'd learned the hard way that nobody should have to live that way. And seeing the joy on her face, he was thrown back into his own memories of the day he'd given up on all that and embraced what he truly was. The teeming wall of microbiota at the lakeshore, the bullies curled up on the ground and moaning as they cradled their own guts, the shock on his friends' faces as the clouds that had risen from the trash bin and the nearby birch copse and the lake itself had converged, coalescing in a fog that surrounded the trio of troublemakers. But, he reminded himself, this wasn't that place, or that time, and Soo-jin wasn't him. He looked at her again, terrified about what was going to happen to her now, here, in this society.

Catching his eye, Soo-jin realized what he must be thinking, and all at once it hit her in a wave of panic: her life as she'd known it was over now. But she didn't waver in her focus: all the test-taking and all the mask-wearing and the frightening warnings, they'd taught her how to handle terror: she let it rush through her, the way the wind rushed through her hair.

Gazing down upon the city from an even greater height, she saw none of the grime, none of the trash and dilapidated buildings. She was struck, instead, by the beauty that distance revealed: the tiny cars and trucks moving along miniature roads, the minibuses hurrying from place to place like mites, and the myriad little figures each following its path on the sidewalk had all seemed so dull and quotidian before. Now, she saw them all with new eyes, and—literally—from a radically new angle. All this had flourished around her for so many years, unrecognized but ever-present. And she had hidden herself amid it all, never realizing her sojourn there would only be temporary. Seeing the world this way, and knowing she could never go back to hiding herself down there, she took a sort of comfort that was inexpressible for her even in her native language.

Soo-jin knew that soon, they would have to decide where to go, what to do. That Trevor Teacher was going to be in trouble, and her parents would be too. That she must go to them soon. And that decisions would have to get made, plans laid out very quickly. But she didn't want to go home, not yet. Not while the sensation of flight was so new, so fresh to her. She knew she could fly for the first time once in her life, and she wanted to enjoy it.

"Hey Teacher!" She tightened her grip on his arm as she grinned. She took aim at the first place she could think of that she really wanted to go. Before he could say anything, before she sent them soaring toward it, she cried out with happy abandon, "Watch this!"

Gord Sellar flew from Canada to South Korea at the end of December 2001, and has remained here almost continually since. His writing has appeared in most of the top speculative fiction venues in English, including *Clarkesworld*, *Asimov's Science Fiction*, *Analog Science Fiction & Fact*, *Lightspeed*, and *Interzone*. A finalist for the John W. Campbell Award for Best New Writer in 2009, his work has been translated to Czech, Chinese, Korean, and Italian. He holds an M.A in Creative Writing from Concordia University (Montréal, CA) and is a graduate of the prestigious Clarion West Writers Workshop (2006). Sellar wrote both the musical score and the screenplay for South Korea's first film adaptation of H.P. Lovecraft's work, Jihyun Park's award-winning *The Music of Jo Hyeja* (Brutal Rice Productions, 2011). More recently, Sellar and Park have made important contributions to the translation of Korean science fiction, contributing several story co-translations to the first English-language anthology of South Korean SF, *Readymade Bodhisattva* (Kaya Press, 2019) and serving as not just contributors to, but also among the consultants, advisors, and liaisons for, the 2019 Clarkesworld Korean SF translation project. Visit his website at gordsellar.com.

Copyright Acknowledgements